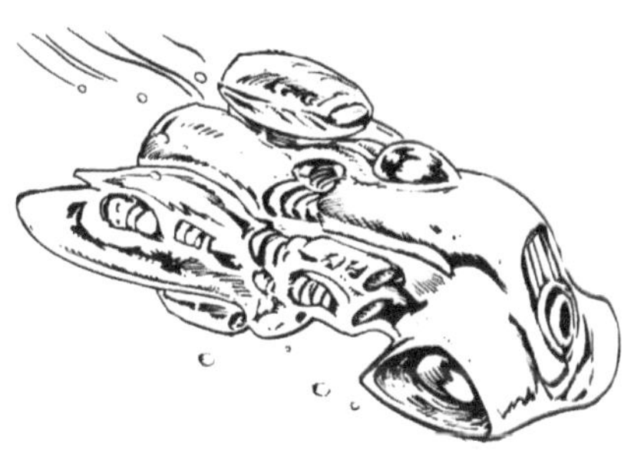

XYZZY

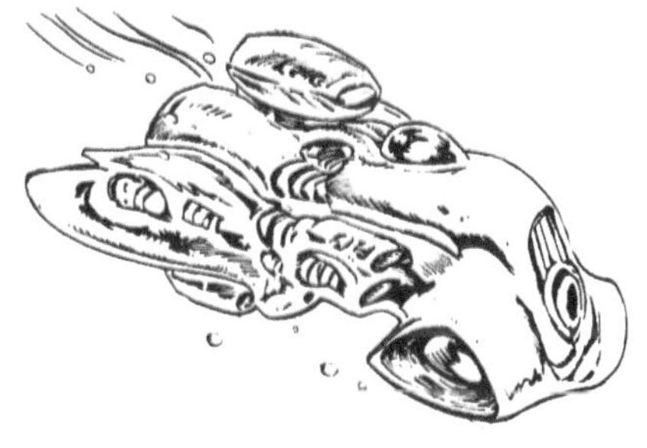

WRITTEN BY:
ODDNESS

ILLUSTRATED BY:
MIKE DUBISCH

XYZZY

SECOND EDITION NOVEMBER 2023
ODDNESS

HARDBACK ISBN: 978-1-960213-31-0
ELECTRONIC ISBN: 978-1-960213-32-7

ALL ARTWORK BY MIKE DUBISCH
NUREMBERG UFO BATTLE BY UNKNOWN AUTHOR, LAYOUT AND EDIT BY ODDNESS

ORDERING INFORMATION:
INFO@ODDNESS.US

WWW.ODDNESS.US

XYZZY

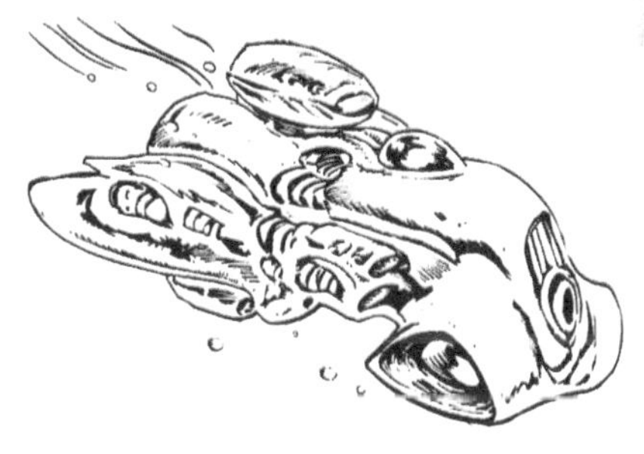

WRITTEN BY:
ODDNESS

ILLUSTRATED BY:
MIKE DUBISCH

1

ALWAYS CLEAN YOURSELF BEFORE DONNING A SPACE SUIT!

The Hugmoun carved a path through the Oort cloud, leaving a trail of shattered crystals in the grand vessel's wake. The pilot inside, Xotro, was tormented by the incessant jarring from the constant bombardment of rocks. Dull clanging thuds shook virtually every corner of the ship. Despite his best efforts to drown out the non-rhythmic reverberations, he knew that his respite would only be at hand once he finally reached the celestial womb whose incubating primates were still living comfortably within the protective nest of trillions of ice-balls and asteroids.

Xotro, the Lead Agent of the Protocol's Second Arm, was a jack-of-all-trades. For him, the years ticked by rapidly, as his people lived for over twenty thousand years on average. His past was an ever-fleeting collection of billions of disappointing memories he hoped to forget as he cruised through space alone in his ship.

He had come back to check on four subordinate Agents who had been stationed on this desolate rock more than a thousand years ago. They were highly proficient in technology assimilation, and Xotro expected much of them, though he couldn't remember much else about the Agents after this long. The lack of an incoming status signal dashed his hopes for a quick and easy visit to Earth.

"I find the quality of these Agents to be rather suspect," Xotro grumbled. His scowling red face grew even redder, and his pair of curled black horns darkened even blacker in frustration. He kicked his hooved feet angrily against the console as he sulked back in his chair. He was clearly in a snit.

The Hugmoun long-range hauler, which he had nicknamed 'Hug' for short, soon passed the outer gas giants of the solar system and proceeded through the last gauntlet of debris between him and his destination—the green and blue planet.

Meanwhile, Hug—filled with all sorts of technological goodies that Xotro was bringing for the Earthlings—mined the nearby asteroid belts with sensor bombs and seeded the solar system with surveillance satellites and defensive automated gun platforms as the massive Xot hauler rapidly closed the gap to Earth.

Xotro often asked himself why he'd spent the past three thousand years running around this backwater sector of the galaxy. The species here were so primitive, and he hadn't seen a single planet he liked. His responding philosophy, however, was simple. Look towards the big picture, don't care about anything else, and always move on. He had to be vigilant as the Lead Agent of the Second Arm. He needed to stay clear-headed and cautious to counter the invading Horde properly. After all, this would be his last chance to prove himself.

The enemy Horde was a loose collection of angry, jealous, and greedy Level Three tribes who periodically stormed together throughout civilized space. Their unsophisticated minds, churning and burning with envy and desire, drove them to loot and pillage weaker planets of all their worth. They had malicious intentions to devour and destroy all people or concepts too alien for them—entire planets' civilizations were wiped out. Files were destroyed, libraries torched, and artwork smashed and shredded.

In addition, simply destroying the cultures of their victims wasn't enough. During every planetary invasion, the unlucky populace would be consumed or conscripted. Cruel Horde scientists replaced the victims' brains with a 'slave-core' that forced them into servitude as mindless foot soldiers. In leaner times, fresh captives were savagely butchered and merely served as foodstuffs for the giant, more aggressive slaves.

It had been hypothesized that perhaps the origin of the Horde's madness was their crude attempts to fuse alien species' body parts to enhance their biological construct in their endless endeavor to augment their ability to endure the physiological rigors of space. The poorly executed organ transplants and transfusions commonly led to tissue rejection or blood poisoning, and very often, some degree of insanity came along with it.

The Hugmoun maintained an orbit around the dark side of the Earth's moon as it searched for any sign of the missing Agents and analyzed the planet's defenses. Hug's samplers were directed to survey all known data streams in search of evidence of alien telecommunications. The ship's transmission feed system was blasted by static and random atmospheric noise. The din grated on Xotro's ears as Hug continued combing the spectrum of surrounding wavelengths for any foreign tidbits of sound or non-native signal. The computer beeped gently as it completed surveilling the planet's defensive grid.

"No appropriate defensive capabilities present," stated Hug. "Five thousand satellites. Nine million five hundred thousand pieces of space junk. One orbital platform. Earthlings are the only remotely intelligent life."

"This zorking planet is naked. Zob blam, it," Xotro muttered incoherently to the ship's console. He thought of the ship's artificial intelligence as a verbal punching bag. He often let loose his frustrations on the inanimate console, as his long service cooped up in the vessel made for a lonely existence.

"No chance of their survival against the Horde, Hug. It will take more than a century to properly buttress the defensive capabilities of this planet. I know younglings that have kits at home more complex than the Earthlings' most advanced particle accelerator."

"Report submitted," informed Hug. The ship's extreme plus-light speed transmitter sent Xotro's report from one arm of the Milky Way Galaxy to another instantly. After the message was received, the long-distance operator shortly returned a transmission that the information was under review and that the Lead Agent was to wait for orders.

The Xots weren't the only visitors to Earth, but presently, the planet was under their protection, so other space-faring folks tended to keep their distance. They did so, especially after the first great conflict between the Xots and a rival extraterrestrial race over a large sub-continent of Earth. The destructive craft battle, witnessed by the awed humans from the ground, had resulted in not only Xot victory but a thin layer of iridium that clouded out the warm, nurturing light of their sun. This was the first of modern man's significant weather-based setbacks, as the ensuing small ice age sent the humans hiding back in their caves for centuries, unable to progress until the environment became favorable enough once more.

The Level Five species made it a point to never mix with any species of such a low advancement level, preferring to allow the primitive peoples of the universe to naturally develop on their own until they were ready for actual intergalactic contact. Consequently, the Xots filled the void of benevolence that was otherwise missing in an indifferent and cold arm of the galaxy, which the Horde had been systematically rampaging through.

The Xots initially planned to advance the human civilization from their basic Level One to about Level Three in less than five hundred years. The plan's first step to initiate contact was to implant advanced circuitry on the planet. They coded this information in ancient enigmas, the goal of which was to advance the target peoples' technological and cultural intelligence to make them more receptive to an eventual in-person Xot visit.

The Xots left many of these puzzles in various places on Earth several times throughout the development of different human civilizations. Unfortunately, the primitive apes that populated the planet did not offer reasonable responses to the cognitive tests; instead, they had an annoying habit of building large stone structures over the templates for the puzzles. It started with Stonehenge and the various pyramids or ziggurats, then Angkor Wat and Machu Picchu. The list of failed opportunities went on and on. Now, direct action was required because the impending threat of the Horde was finally all too real. There was no more time to wait or play games.

"There will be no more babysitting of these apes. This last planet cannot fail. It's too close to the nearest onramp of the intergalactic transdimensional expressway," growled the irritated Xotro.

For Earth to fall under Horde influence would jeopardize the Xot Empire and the lives of all living beings whose planets orbited near the transit lines of the expressway. There was too much at stake.

2

FOLLOW, BROTHERS. ONLY RUN SLOWER SO MY ENEMY MAY KNOW YOU AS WELL AS I DO.

The blinking message on the yellow console screen was unmistakable. All Protocol Agents were familiar with it, just as they knew the grooves of the mood moderator chips lodged in their spine.

Hug repeated the blinking message, 'Xokar.'

Xokar was a command translated as 'face the tidal wave,'under the Xot Empire's high order, Xotro was expected to aid the Earthlings in their fight against the Horde wave—until victory or until the bitter end.

"It's not my fault the planet isn't advanced enough," Xotro intoned as his mood grew fouler. "Why am I stuck with this ape rock?"

Xotro's first step was to locate any living Agents, hear their briefings, and then he could proceed to contact the strongest world leaders about the imminent Horde invasion. Actually, he didn't really even need the Earth's leaders; he simply required about five hundred thousand skilled pilots. He would train them to fight against the alien swarm, and that would be it. There was no time for other options. Xotro was the closer in this deal, and he alone was to handle the negotiations, though he had no real cultural context from which to draw to work out the finer points of the deal.

"You know, Hug, the Earthlings are on the cusp of Level Two... They're pretty close," Xotro commented as he flicked through different images and documents Hug pulled up for him through the humans' World Wide Web.

He could see that the apes were just beginning to make rudimentary strides in space exploration and nanotechnology. The primates were not without flaws, though, clearly seen from the grossly wasteful and violent nature of the species.

"Still, their in-fighting, improper allocation of resources, unsustainable sourcing practices, and lack of a united world government will eventually be their downfall. It's still so easy for these apes to fail on so many levels. How can I really be expected to actually help save them?"

Xotro sighed. To be charged with aiding the humans against the Horde was to be charged with a nearly impossible task. There just wasn't enough time, but there was no arguing with it.

"...that won't be our problem, Hug. I'll be long gone by then and with a full stomach."

Xotro rubbed his empty belly and continued to think of food for just a few more minutes after talking to his ship's computer. The only things he'd been eating for the past year, since his last supply pit stop, were cheaply flavored tubes of hydrated nutrient goo. While the artificial flavoring was awful, it served a purpose to partially cover up the harsh metallic and bitter tastes of the concentrated minerals and vitamins. The gritty paste was very unpleasant to ingest, and as he hungrily groped through his snack cupboard, he realized that he had just run out of the flavored ones. The old expired packs of original flavor tubes stared at Xotro from the back of the cupboard. He slammed the cabinet door shut grumpily; he might as well be licking Hug's exhaust pipes. He trudged back to his captain's chair and plopped himself down heavily. No Agents, no time to prepare for the Horde, and no edible food. The day was just not going his way.

Hug continued to process the planet's information infrastructure, digesting and analyzing the data for any Protocol reference or Xot signature, searching for clues as to the whereabouts of the missing Agents. No relevant data was gleaned from the files that Hug continued to compile for review by

Xotro. The computer dug further into the information until it finally noticed a company with a very distinctive visual as its logo; it was clearly the Xot character for zero, with the name GAMElab stylized in block letters underneath.

"Agent Zero's headquarters located!" chimed Hug cheerily.

"Lock in the coordinates and prepare my scout ship for its departure," he instructed Hug.

Xotro was concerned about the Horde situation, but not for the sake of the simple beings who called this region of the galaxy home. The risk that the enemy imposed on the intergalactic expressway was a much bigger deal. He was cavalier about the humans' chances of surviving the attack, as he was worried more about his reputation than having any genuine concern for some backwoods apes. He didn't want to live another few thousand more years being reminded of his failures as the worst Lead Agent in Xot history. The idea of such a disgrace burned in his skull.

Xotro boarded the scout ship and burst into the lower troposphere, breaking the sound barrier. The landing was accompanied by a sonic boom echoing from high above for miles. His small craft settled on a clearing in an old-growth redwood forest of northern California. He made sure no one was hanging around or watching him before he hopped out of his ship.

Xotro took necessary precautions because if the Agent was AWOL, his visit might be resented by the long-lost Agent. He still had a blaster if needed, but Xots didn't kill other Xots; they resorted to subterfuge. For example, it wasn't uncommon for a Xot to be drugged and incapacitated after consuming the contents of a welcoming Grek platter soon after a friendly visit. The motivations of such deceptions were seldom clear, as after living thousands of years, you were bound to forget more than a few grudge-holding enemies from your past.

The walk up the grassy hill towards the building was swift and uneventful. The sound of insects chirping like elevator muzak in the background suddenly stopped as he approached, starting up again a few moments after he passed by. The house he inspected was a large compound with multiple wings. Agent Zero had designed an excellent place for himself.

The building's architecture was very similar to the Xot communal housing style, and it looked smartly futuristic, at least by human standards. Familiar translucent gates, self-adjusting solar panels, twisting columns, and swooping contours greeted Xotro's homesick eyes. Along with the telltale logo on the front, it was clear that a Xot lived inside. In addition, up until then, no biological attack beasts or beam cameras had targeted him, which was good. The only thing left was simply gaining entry into the building.

Fifteen feet from the western side of the house, Xotro boosted himself to the roof with a leap from his powerful thighs. He tiptoed across, looking for the typical Xot landing pad, which traditionally had an entry hatch. This would be his way into the building. To the untrained eye, it looked like a mere roof vent; to the trained eye, it was an unnecessary vent. To the Xot, it was a passage that led to the center of the house, where usually a spherical flying pod was parked for the host, which provided entry to any room that could be reached from the central area.

Xotro slinked down the passage, being careful to avoid any possible traps. His entrance to the central room was, again, uneventful. The room was filled with blue light that reflected from the Xot devices littering the chamber. It was an extensive research laboratory instead of a pod garage. Xotro spied on the long-range communicator, which was clearly being repaired. Various experimental devices also filled the room. Contraptions that were a combination of Xot and native technology cluttered the countertops and desks and were likely adapted for native use. While looking at all the miscellaneous pieces of plastic and metal scrap and computer chips, Xotro figured that Agent Zero must at least have an alarm system that had been triggered when he entered the compound. He ought to be seeing the Agent very soon.

As these thoughts passed, a Xot burst into the room. He was holding a trident blaster aimed at the ready. When he was through with all the bluster, however, he stopped and stood straight at attention because he recognized Xotro.

"Sir, Agent Zero reporting for duty, Sir!" he announced loudly as he saluted the Lead Agent.

Xotro remembered this Agent now—a talkative, annoyingly bright-eyed, idealistic youth.

"Do you have my report, Agent Zero?"

"Sir, not yet, Sir! It will take a couple of hours to compile, Sir!"

"At ease, Agent." Xotro waved his hand, motioning for the Agent to relax his stiff formalities. "Is there anyone else in the house?"

"No, Sir," replied Agent Zero in a more casual voice, setting the trident blaster down to lean against a nearby table.

"Any other Agents alive?"

"Yes, Sir. Just one more. The other two are dead."

Hearing that half of the Agents had died since their deployment only a millennium ago was a little bit of a surprise. "Who is still alive?" Xotro asked.

"Just Agent One, Sir."

"How did the other Agents die?"

"In my report, the context will make more sense, but as a direct answer to your question, most recently, Agent 3.14 died on Earth in 1906 while on a mission to the country of Russia. His assignment was to monitor scientific developments and to assist anywhere that he could do so surreptitiously. The Russians, at the turn of the century, were making remarkable strides in physics and maintained a popular notion that life existed on other planets. They seemed to be our perfect candidates. Unfortunately, his scout ship exploded in the lower atmosphere and flattened the nearby Tunguska Woods. Everything was vaporized. Humans assumed it to be a meteorite exploding in the upper atmosphere that showered the ground below, leveling the entire forest. The bang was heard around the world."

"Why did the ship explode?"

"Sir, it was probably due to poor preventative maintenance. He always did a half-assed job. His craft was always breaking down."

"Enough," demanded Xotro, tired of hearing about the dead Agent's incompetence. "Feed me now. I'm starving. Then, start from the beginning of your mission, and please skip the usual boring statistics."

"Yes, Sir. I'll be right back."

"Leave the blaster tube," suggested Xotro.

Agent Zero nodded and was gone for about ten minutes before he returned with a platter of delicacies: a bowl and open bottles of processed fizzy sugar water, a plate of lactate slices, and assorted live rodents in a glass feeding ball, with tongs to pick them up with.

Xotro enjoyed practicing Grek when he was off-world. For him, it was the only real perk of traveling. Grek was a time-honored tradition in which the host provided a fresh meal to the weary guest, who'd previously been sustained by freeze-dried ground rodent meat and the ubiquitous space-faring staple of nutritive goo tubes. If off-world, the host provided suitable local ingredients in an otherwise traditionally prepared Xot meal. The native substitutions were still considered a delicacy to be savored and enjoyed by both the host and guest, with the traveler moving on after the platter was consumed. Since Agent Zero was the host, he ate the first bites in a ritualistic display, as per custom, to show that the food was not drugged, and then proceeded to introduce Xotro to the local refreshments.

Agent Zero, with a wide toothy grin, took a bright slice of cheese product and fished out a live hamster with the tongs, wrapped the cheese around it in a fluid motion, and dipped the struggling roll into the bowl. The pop into his mouth was fast, and he was chewing the creamy, meaty assortment with his extended mouth open very wide in demonstration. Feet and tail with bits of golden cheese were the last sightings of the food that drained down his throat.

The mere sight and smell of the mouthwatering hors d'oeuvres had worked up an intense appetite in Xotro, and he couldn't wait to dig in, convinced of the delicious taste. He felt comfortable, and soon, both men were seated, eating their finger food and enjoying a real feast.

Agent Zero spoke to his leader in a friendly manner. "I'm sure you will enjoy this Earth delicacy. It's called cheese. It is made of the enzymatically-treated coagulated milk fats and proteins of Earth bovines. Do you like it?"

Xotro responded by continuing to eat heartily. His silence was the acknowledgment of the tasty treat. Rodents were rodents on any planet, but the smooth slices of savory fermented animal by-product definitely served to elevate the flavor. The particularly hairy rodents of Earth he had to adjust to, though. While the flavor was terrific, the texture of the furry animal being swallowed gave him the feeling of a giant toothbrush scrubbing down his throat.

"The sharp, fizzy dipping sauce is a popular local beverage—a high-calorie carbohydrate syrup perfect for our needs. The Earthlings make many versions of this drink, flavored with various aromatic compounds. This one is called 'root beer.' The added carbonation replaces the bacterial metabolic gases from the decaying bladders of the Drukian canine. I no longer have to run a decomp factory in my lab."

"Agent Zero, start with the mission's inception," said Xotro as he dabbled with an improvised method of gluttony, taking swigs of root beer from the bubbling bottle and dropping a squeaking mouse into his mouth.

"Yes, Sir! The landing party had arrived on Earth during its latest round of the Dark Ages. When we landed, we still bore our natural appearance—the red skin, horns, and tail, equipped with the tri-tip blaster tube, as protocol dictated. We scared the hell out of the locals, unfortunately. They pelted us with stones and chased us back to our ship. Our encounter was subsequently chronicled in several medieval paintings that depicted our scout craft and our image." Agent Zero pointed to the monitor, where the computer presented images corresponding to his talk. Meanwhile, high-pitched squealing and small bones crunching continued in the background.

"Progress was held up by minor ice ages and cold periods triggered by solar variance. While in disguise, we took shelter in an abandoned religious institution called a monastery. We helped spark their long road to recovery, or as they called it, 'The Renaissance.' We sprinkled information around the continent, and soon, their technical, scientific, and artistic skills began blossoming. For example, regarding the relationship between a piece of art and the viewer, they made the simple shift from presenting a central fixed image to providing a more enlightening experience in transforming the viewer into the subject of the portrait. For decades, we ran a workshop in Italy. Raphael was one of our best unknowing proxy Agents, a key player in transforming the merchant class. Alas, he failed to break the humans of their deititial awe."

Xotro was impatient. He didn't care for history because the answer was always in the moment. Also, the history of humans was utterly immaterial to the situation. He let Agent Zero complete his report instead of interrupting him, however, as he had delicious fresh food.

"Out of the worst of it, we fought off the invasion of the Cruszarin Flow—the convoy of dilapidated cruise liners searching for planets to leech. We battled them over the skies of Nuremberg and handily prevented them from making this planet their port of call."

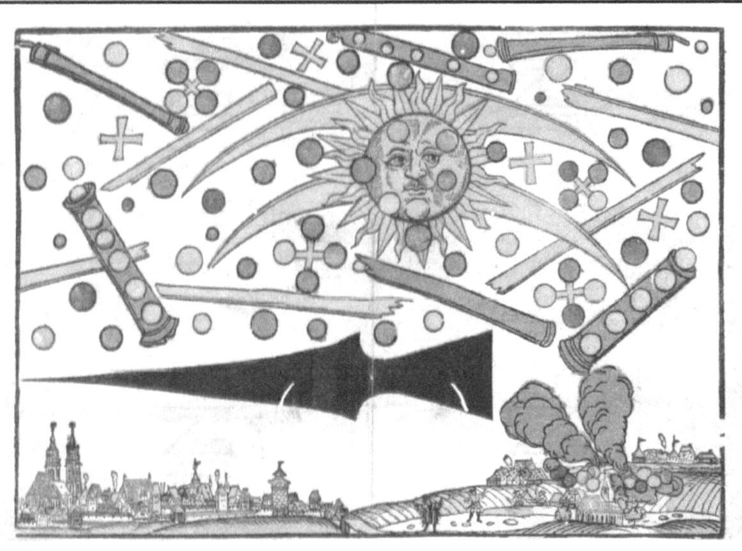

"...the Trot's testicles really got rolling in the last century! The planet's greatest milestones were achieved in the shortest amount of time! Fuel-based engines, a worldwide network of computers, nuclear power, satellites, and orbiting spacecraft were technological advancements born of war. They even got to the moon! But the humans don't have a chance of facing off with the Horde; even the most advanced civilization can succumb to barbarians when hopelessly outnumbered or outgunned."

Agent Zero paused again as Xotro polished off the last rodent wraps from the fifth Grek platter. He handed Xotro another drink to wash it down and waited to allow Xotro time to pick the bones from his teeth and wipe his bare chest free of food grizz.

"Do forgive me, Xotro. Now I will continue," said Agent Zero.

He used his tongue to lick his lips, now feeling dry from all the talking he'd done. They were still a little sweet from the soda. He took a sip of the root beer to moisten his throat and went on.

"Agent 6.28 was unbalanced from the beginning. He went from slightly odd and somewhat bearable to utterly stark, raving mad. That was about halfway through the mission. He was never directly seen again, although we did see something of his doing pop up in a book entitled 'Dante's Inferno,' as it contained crude depictions of our hive chambers on Xot. Unfortunately, the Inquisition, a human fear-based termination squad, stepped in to silence those he had influenced, and science met with a wall. In conclusion, progress was effectively halted until this last century."

Xotro was relieved that the report on the worthless deceased Agents was finally complete. Time was limited, and his options were relatively few on this backwater planet.

"Let's meet Agent One. I'd like to hear his zorking side of the story," Xotro said as he gestured towards the central chamber.

The two prepared their things and started for the door. Half-way there, the Lead Agent paused in mid-stride with a sudden thought. He was feeling pretty full by now, but he didn't want to get hungry later.

"And Agent Zero, pack some Grek platters for the trip!"

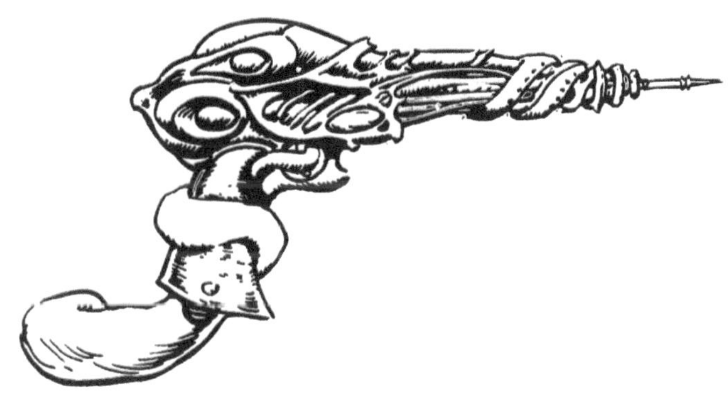

3

WHEN YOU GRAB REZO'S NUT SACK, IT SCREAMS.

Agent Zero's arms were overloaded with supplies for Xotro's Grek platters. He cumbersomely followed Xotro into the cockpit of the scout ship. It was just about time to depart to where Agent One was stationed in the underground secret base outside Washington, D.C. He called in to let Agent One know they were coming and then sat down exhaustedly in the cabin. He was tired from all his research and preparations and would catch a quick nap while Xotro flew like they had planned beforehand.

"Agent Zero, are you forgetting something?" asked Xotro in a firm voice. "Keep me awake... Finish your briefing."

Agent Zero opened his eyes and turned to Xotro. He didn't remember where he'd left off with the briefing of his work on Earth but started with the most critical section.

"As I mentioned, Sir, the gaming platform was the training program needed to hone the lifelong skills necessary to pilot the Xorts in skilled combat," he said in tired, clipped tones.

"Oh, be quiet. You're boring me already," the leader groaned. "Your only concern now is to formulate a plan that helps us meet the protocol's objectives to prep the humans to battle the Horde. You are most familiar with this planet, so go. You know what to do."

"But Sir, the program—" Agent Zero tried to interject.

"Go now and prepare the reports, and by all means, fly the craft. I have some eating to do," said Xotro with a lazy yawn.

Xotro stumbled to the back of the cabin, slumped into the plush, easy chair, and pulled the packed lunch boxes over to his seat. He continued to eat until he'd demolished a second Grek platter. Then he passed out.

Naturally, hours later, Xotro stumbled out of his food coma, and he was angry. He'd just slept through two hours of the trip.

"Agent Zero, you have wasted too much time already!" he shouted. "I want you to write the contact speech of how the planet is zorked and how we will help the apes, and so on and so forth. You disappoint me; you should have anticipated my needs! Where is the fresh Grek platter? Get this done now before we land!"

"The Horde mass has reached Pluto...." The ship's voice trailed in the background, ignored by the leader.

"But Sir—" Agent Zero was cut off again by Xotro's wayward glance over one of the viewing screens.

Bored with Agent Zero, Xotro started watching the Earthlings' charming informational programs. He could understand what the humans in the program were talking about, thanks to the translating capabilities of his spinal mood moderator chip. They appeared to be advertisements for various useless Earth products. Still, the short clips of comical scenes, bright colors, and music amused Xotro, as the twenty-second or so commercials were a perfect length for his short attention span. He made himself comfy and once again fell into a deep slumber on the easy chair of the scout ship, hands resting on his plumped belly.

Agent Zero had already drafted a speech to address the people of Earth, using his knowledge of their culture while simultaneously multitasking to pilot the ship and maintain watch throughout their flight. The major challenge of the speech was the Xot language and the two hundred-plus Earth languages whose syntax and vocabularies did not mesh conveniently in their chip's translation matrix—something he had learned long ago during his many years of living here. The so-called Universal Grammar wasn't doing him any favors.

He gazed out the cockpit at the city lights glimmering below as he flew the ship overhead. The clearing to the secret underground base on the East Coast was somewhat hidden in a muddy riverside park just on the outskirts of the capital. Agent Zero was glad he had pushed old Woody to get it established back during the country's entry into the Great War. It had been established during wartime as a convenient means to store confidential technologies under development. It had sophisticated communications devices to contact the United Nations and other allies and countries all over the globe.

"Sir, we have the connection, and the networks are under our control," reported Agent Zero.

"Uh, what?" muttered Xotro, still trying to listen to the shows in his sleep. He was oblivious as the craft rumbled to a stop, and the Agent parked it at their destination. "Any food on this flight?" Xotro asked, smacking his lips.

"Sir, the remains of your Grek platter are on your left. We're in the landing bay of the secret base outside this country's capital," informed Agent Zero, turning off the ship's thrusters. "You have access to their information channels. The switch inside activates the live signal."

Xotro dismissed Agent Zero and then finished off the rest of his platter, licking some of the cheese smears from the plate. "In-flight meals are never as appetizing. The cafeteria here better be good, Agent."

They exited the scout ship and entered the bay of the underground base. Xotro saw that the room was vast and had a high ceiling, big enough to hold many large aircraft. Monitors covered all the walls, and he found they were already linked with the external elements at his command. Several screens displayed in numerous angles that the Horde was currently held at the cluster of ice dwarves around Pluto.

The gun platforms Xotro had left behind during his flight towards Earth had caught them off guard and wreaked havoc on the central beast of the swarm—the Horde Mothership—and had targeted other critical areas in their ranks so that the Horde was forced to slow down to regroup and repair damages.

"Ah, I see my diversions are working," he laughed as he ordered the Agents into action. This would buy them much-needed time to prepare the Earthlings.

Agent One had been expecting the pair and had gotten the necessary equipment prepared for them beforehand. Cameras and mics were ready, satellite override jacks were on, and a platter of food and make-up lay on a table nearby.

Xotro walked up to the camera in his full Xot glory, naked, holding the tri-tip blaster tube. He commanded Agent One to give him a full-body grooming in preparation for his address to the entire Earth. As the representative of the Xot people, he had a duty to look his best. He had Agent One buff up his horns and cloven feet to a glossy shine, massage fragrant herbal lotion into his skin, brush his leg fur until smooth and silky, and finally, scrub clean his nether regions. It was a complete Xot makeover.

While Xotro was getting himself dolled up, Agent Zero used the time to establish a powerful Xot override to transmit their message over all channels of human use, taking over both analog and digital signal televisions and radios worldwide. He loaded up the speech he'd written during the flight into Agent One's teleprompter for Xotro to read off of during his address.

He glanced over to see his fellow Agent rubbing down Xotro's derriere with a towel. He felt happy that Agent One was there to wipe Xotro's ass instead of having the demeaning job fall to him, though he felt a little bad for his friend.

At last, Xotro was completely polished and ready to show the Earthlings Xot diplomacy at its finest. He signaled to Agent Zero to start the live broadcasting in a few moments, and the Agent began a silent countdown with his fingers to allow the leader to prepare. Xotro stood tall, cleared his throat loudly, and faced the camera. Then it was three, two, one, and action.

"People of Earth," he began slowly, "as you have already observed, a threat looms on the horizon from an extremely hostile enemy that is very intent on destroying all of you..."

Xotro paused awkwardly because he was no longer able to read the teleprompter beside the camera. It had malfunctioned, and the little screen was stuck on the first sentence. Agent One motioned for him to continue improvising while he and Zero scrambled to repair the machine.

"I am Xotro, from the planet Xot. I am here to peacefully love you and your animals and rub my love member on all your people." Despite some struggle with the English vocabulary, he was pleased with delivering his message of love and peace, but now he wanted to make sure that a reward was covered up-front.

"I am also here to help you defend your pathetic selves from the worst nightmares in your dreams. I will rip away the superstitious teddy bear you cling to in your darkest moments with the stupid thoughts that it will rescue you."

Off camera, Agent One was encouraging Xotro to continue while Agent Zero, who had a better grasp of English, bounced up and down, shaking his head back and forth, trying to encourage him to stop. Xotro continued, heartened by Agent One's smiles and waving.

"I have a solution that will help you Earthlings. It is a bargain. It will only cost you in rodents and larger, tasty mammalian forms. There will be a need for many, and they will be for my personal consumption. But no zorking marsupials! They give me gas. Of course, I will require a sampler platter to make any final decisions. I also want two million liters of carbonated liquid—root beer preferred—and two tons of your best processed orange cheese products." He wanted to ensure enough food and drink for the rest of his life; he'd never have to eat another zorking tube of nutrient paste.

Agent Zero pushed Agent One away from the camera, and he caught Xotro's attention, managing to communicate to him to wrap it up quickly. Xotro's awful speech and idiotic demands were too much for him to bear.

"In conclusion, I expect the country leader called 'United States,' to present the nation's most premium representative at the following coordinates by tomorrow at 9 a.m. East Coast standard human time. If not, you may face the threat on your own."

Xotro walked away from the camera as Agent One cut the link to the satellites.

"That was good, wasn't it?" asked Xotro, clearly not aware of everything he had really said.

"Great speech, Xotro!" gushed Agent One.

The humans were all glued to their info cubes. At all times, they were connected to the information network—inside with their TVs and computers, outside, on the sidewalk, browsing with their tablets, or even their phones. The news about the bizarre devil man's questionable bargain spread quickly; he offered protection from an invading alien army in exchange for several metric tons of rats and junk food. All newscasters on any news station were showing either the footage of Xotro's speech or a grainy video showing a hazy cloud venturing toward the outer edges of Pluto's orbital border. The leading scientists from NASA, EOA, and NOAA had been conferring during the past hour to discuss the Hubble Space Telescope's latest shots from the mass identified just hours earlier.

Governments worldwide were shuttling their diplomats to the UNSC—United Nations Security Council—to begin an emergency session called for by the United States. The U.S. was intent on independently verifying the alien's rumor of the dangerous cloud's contents. Strange space phenomena were one thing; a space invasion was another. The unidentified mass had slowed, and the President was getting his tenth report of the day on the subject while he paced by his desk. Sisko, a top-notch secret agent, had just entered the President's chamber, holding a stack of files. He was dressed in a sharp black suit, earpiece, and shades.

The secret Agent was a trusted friend, and he wasted no time informing him of the latest news, as he reported, "Mr. President, the EXCTO satellite has detected a large mass—not completely solid, and definitely not gas. It's been moving irregularly at high speeds, has held its position near the outer ice dwarves for several hours, and has not yet passed Pluto. Faint explosions and light beams have been detected. Speculation is that some sort of energy exchange is happening through the light beams." He placed several folders filled with photos and files concerning the mass onto President Engressia's desk.

The President was sure it was no coincidence that some lame-looking jackass had hijacked the communication satellites and played a disgusting viral joke on everyone across the globe. But weren't pranks like that only supposed to happen on the web? Who ever heard of someone jacking into all the radio broadcasting worldwide? How could that jabbering 'deviled ham' have access to such powerful technology? Chances were that this was no joke, no matter how ridiculous it seemed. The secret Agent's continued briefing soon interrupted his thoughts.

"...and the current trajectory is towards Earth. At its rate of speed, it will reach us within approximately forty-eight hours. It is not a group of asteroids, nor is it a comet swarm. According to NASA, the sighting seems to actually confirm what the..."

Sisko trailed off and looked at the President, who looked back at him expectantly. The image that he was trying to describe just sounded too stupid for words.

He had an audible pause in his speech as he searched for an appropriate word to describe the Xot speaker. "...It, uh, confirms what the 'Devil' reported to us earlier today about an invading extraterrestrial army."

"If that's the case, it's time to open a dialogue with the alien," said the President, "and you are to be the Ambassador, Mr. Sisko, on this great country's—no, this great PLANET'S behalf. I want you to assess the terms of his assistance. Is he earnest about soda pop and rats? I am sure it will cost us much more dearly than that. Certainly, that was just a taste of the demands to come in the future. What exactly is the 'love member'?"

Naturally, the humans watching Xotro's speech had glanced at a particular area on his body upon his usage of the term, but the Xot's region was as smooth and featureless as the crotch of a Ken doll. This made President Engressia all the more anxious as to what the devilish speaker wanted. He held his heavy head in his hands as he spoke to Sisko.

"Depart now, Mr. Sisko, for the most important meeting in the history of Earth."

The two men shook hands, and Sisko was off.

The trip to the coordinates of the secret location was brief and incident-free, as it was very close by. The sun rose, the weather was good, the flight was quick, and then there was a gentle landing. The new Ambassador hoped this was a good omen foreshadowing the negotiations. In the past, he often found that the circumstances preceding a meeting often reflected the outcome. Hectic days led to heated conferences and vice versa. That was why it was vital that he keep a calm and collected head and make sure that negotiations ran smoothly. He drew up his courage and confidence. He had been the point man in countless top-secret missions and pressing global matters, and he had always worked things out safely and efficiently, no matter the conflict or danger. Today should be no different.

The tin building on the isolated landing strip looked like a small, rundown airport traffic control station. He had thought that this old facility had been pretty much stripped down and abandoned after the First World War; apparently, that wasn't the case. The Ambassador descended from the tiny chopper, and the pilot flew away, leaving him alone to speak with the aliens.

A tall, broad figure was waving to him from the entryway of the tin building. Sisko looked around. After seeing no immediate threats, he moved towards the open door. The surly man at the entry was enormous, at least seven feet tall, since he was stooping below the door frame as he slowly backed into a bright room. His head was a mess of curly brown hair, framing a pinched and unpleasant face.

"Enter," directed the tall man.

The Ambassador entered the brightly lit room and saw that it contained a lonely table and chair. That was all. Immediately, the door closed behind him, and the room was filled with a highly brilliant white light that seemed to bleed all the detail from the room. The only sensation he felt was butterflies in his gut, and he gasped for air as the room suddenly dropped at least a hundred feet per second until it reached the bottom of the elevator shaft. Unable to scream, the Ambassador caught his breath and straightened his tie and jacket as his heart raced. His tracking pen was still in place, but the tall, ugly escort was nowhere to be found.

After making a complete stop, the two doors of the elevator slid open to reveal a large room with an assortment of computer banks and high-tech access panels with large screens. The swarm was clearly defined on the largest screen in the rnnm nn the center panel. The other screens were focused on different parts of the swarm or various portions of the solar system. It reminded him of a boss' lair from the Flint super-spy movies. He was shocked that an underground facility of this size and sophistication had been practically invisible under their noses all these years.

Inside the room were also three tall Xots who resembled the devil speaker of the hijacked message. They were standing side by side, facing the Ambassador with oversized smiles, which showed off their sharp, pearly teeth. They were trying to appear friendly and welcoming to the Ambassador, but the forced grimaces they bore would have made children cry.

"Plcasc come in, visitor. Don't bother looking for your guide. He was a hologram. Join us over here by the control console. I want to show you something," offered Agent Zero.

"Wait," barked Xotro to everyone in the room, "let him introduce himself first."

The Ambassador walked over. The closer he got, the more detail he could see from the various panels. The amber light of a complex hologram displayed the entire Milky Way Galaxy in a gorgeous mid-air spectacle. He stopped to stare at the scene in awe.

"Fooled by shadows, ape?" Xotro laughed. "Come closer, Earthling, no more tricks. I have a story to tell you. But no questions for now; it would only delay matters. My name is Xotro," he said as he leaned in, waiting for a reply.

"My name is Ambassa—" Sisko managed to sputter before he was cut off.

"Assador? Great to meet you," said Xotro, talking over him. "Strong name. I like that," he complimented as he put his apple-red arm around the Ambassador and led him towards a large desk. "Walk this way, Assador."

The Ambassador didn't bother with corrections. He stood next to the table as the Xot leader began speaking.

Xotro spoke slowly and clearly as he described the local governance structure of this branch of the Milky Way Galaxy, lest he confuse the poor Earth ape with all his advanced talk.

"You see, my planet Xot is responsible for assisting Level One and Two planets when threatened by the Horde. Our goal is threefold: first, awareness of the galaxy; second, acceleration; and third, acceptance into the great Xot Empire. We all face the same threat from those space barbarians, whether a Level One or a Level Five race. The Horde is a disgusting, loose collection of tribes that grew over time into the enormous ravaging army they are now. They came together, gobbling up planet after planet, consuming all natural resources, killing the natives, and stealing any useful technology before moving on to the next planet. Just look at this map, Assador."

Xotro pointed to the center of the local arm of the galaxy, which displayed several strings of blue arrows. One lone white arrow stood at the end of all the blue in a familiar-looking star system.

"The blue arrows are dead worlds, already destroyed by the Horde. The white one is Earth. The string of planets here was either Level One or Two, incapable of fighting off the Horde of invaders. Your planet is still Level One-ish—not quite Level Two status, technically. So-so progress, you know. All the populated planets so far have been totally razed by the Horde, and they're presently heading for Earth. In each case, the barbarians were attracted by the noisy broadcast of each planet, which they sniffed out like bloodthirsty parasites. All the radio and television signals you apes have been using the act as a big 'we are here beacon' for the Horde. Soon, we realized that the only way to protect this planet was to actively accelerate the natives' defense capabilities."

The Ambassador was astonished, and with nothing to say, he merely looked on as the Xot speaker continued his history lesson that related how and why each system had inevitably fallen. Sisko could feel Xotro's build-up to the pitch in the old defense industry rant about protection and the need for arms. He could tell that Xotro had given this speech many times before, too, most likely to the peoples of the fallen worlds on the map marked with the ominous blue arrows. He silently wondered why none of the other planets nearby had survived, even with the Xot's help.

Xotro continued his rant, finishing up with an explanation of Horde migration patterns and the hows and whys of why Earth was positioned at an unfortunate convergence point for the barbarians' massing, where the Horde was planning to regroup its entire army after its numerous campaigns through this branch of the galaxy.

"Your planet, the last standing in this arm, will be protected under our ancient Xot guidance. We need to defend this particular region of the local galaxy from any more destruction."

Ambassador Sisko was waiting for the catch—the price. This was a dire war situation, and he was confident they would have to pay dearly for the aliens' help.

"We only need you to defend your planet and hold the line. It will cost you nothing but lives and the terms that I dictated in my speech to the planet," Xotro said offhandedly.

"Our lives?" queried the Ambassador.

Xotro nodded. "You misunderstand me. I bring fighter crafts to combat the invading Horde. Your people only need to pilot the crafts staff the guns, and, of course, follow my military leadership during the battle. That is the price."

"Ah, well, uh, I believe I will have to speak with the President about this," the Ambassador explained. He couldn't agree to terms like that without discussing it first. "And also, how do you expect our pilots to even fly these foreign spacecraft? At the very least, we would need a demonstration."

"Assador, I expected as much! I have a pad here with information outlining what you need to do to prepare. Just follow the directions and meet us here tomorrow at sunrise," ordered Xotro, patting Sisko jovially on the back. "We will be ready to train your men then."

"Understood. I will do that. However, first, do you really want root beer, processed cheese, and rodents?" Sisko had to ask.

"Enough questions! I don't joke, and the specifications are on the pad, Assador!" Xotro was losing his temper, and he hurried the Ambassador back towards the elevator, pad in hand.

Sisko walked into the elevator while gripping the electronic pad securely, preparing for the rush back up to ground level. Though relieved that he was done talking to the creepy-looking aliens, he began to have a bad feeling gnaw at the back of his mind as he reflected on the day's events. The doors closed quickly. The last glimpse he had of the three was of their wide, toothy grins as they tried to politely wave goodbye.

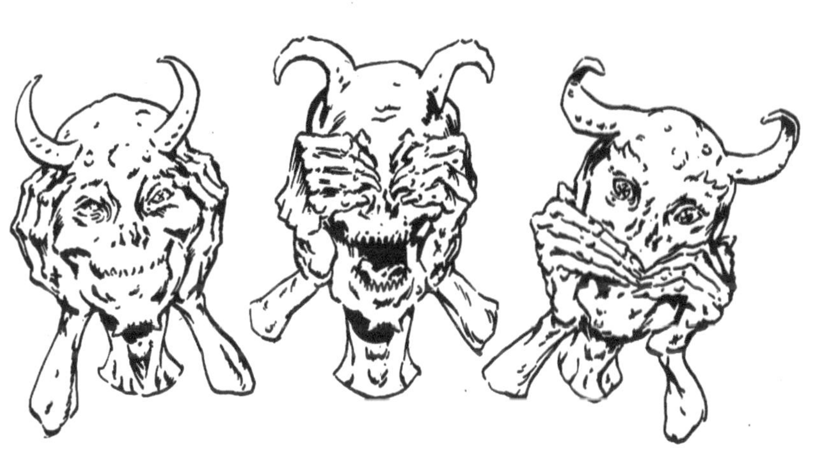

4

THE MOON SETS WHEN IT PASSES THE HORIZON.

The following day, a little after dawn, a convoy of trailers, military vehicles, and a flotilla of cargo helicopters arrived at the time that had been specified. They were full of hundreds of trained soldiers from the U.S. Air Force—the lives that Xotro had asked for. The drone of propellers and engines, the skeptical mumbling of the pilots, and the shouts of commanders filled the booming soundscape.

Agent One stepped forward to meet Ambassador Sisko, who was today followed by a team of military brass. The soldiers had their orders, and so, a long series of buildings, half cylinder-shaped, were being assembled in orderly rows all along the landing strip. Power and communication cables were piped into each of the buildings. Once built, the doors were opened, and pallets of unmarked boxes were carted into the rooms.

Agent Zero observed the proceedings and answered questions. Meanwhile, Xotro and Agent One led the Ambassador and his team into the elevator, and they were quickly transported downward. The Ambassador said nothing as the floor dropped and the door to the control room opened. Collectively, the brass was a little shaken by the ride but not too stirred, still wondering if all the alien spaceship talk was for real.

"This is command central, where I, Xotro, will direct the battle. A series of automated mobile observation posts have been cleverly installed by me throughout the solar system, giving us a nearly unlimited viewpoint of the enemy's movements," Xotro explained in his little tour of the room.

"So, what—" the General was cut off.

"Hold all questions until the end," interjected Agent One.

"Normally, a planet's defense force must be deployed manually with actual pilots. Our scientists have fashioned a specialized defensive system that only requires a neural connection to pilot the Xort ships and the guns, allowing the user to remotely control the ship from anywhere, saving valuable time and supplies otherwise wasted in transportation, gearing up, and boarding."

Xotro looked around the room at the speechless humans. They seemed to be having a hard time believing what they were hearing. They would get their demo shortly and see what was what.

"You Earthlings will steer the Xort using our advanced piloting systems, which are currently being installed in the buildings above us. And as for the demonstration, please watch the screen. It's like flying a drone—a concept you apes can thank us Xots for."

The soldiers didn't like the snobby tone that Xotro used with them, but they held their tongues as they watched the alien presentation.

Agent One sat at a piloting station nearby and fiddled with the controls. Within a few minutes, he was plugged in and manning a single noninvasive Xort via Remote Pilot Station, or RPS. On the screen before them, the men saw a long silver triangle. The ship was sleek and sexy, and all of the features one would expect to find on an aircraft, such as the cockpit, doors, or engines, were invisible. Nothing marred the smooth chrome finish—not one single seam.

"Gentlemen," Agent One began, "you are watching the Xort. Each craft has visual and audio transmission capabilities. It is versatile, has state-of-the-art cloaking shields, and can be used as a scouting or patrol tool."

The Xort skimmed across the moon's surface, leaving behind a thick trail of white dust. It made some twists and turns and other fancy looping maneuvers and then headed straight for Earth. The air marshal and his men were largely unimpressed and still doubtful so far, as they had only seen what could merely be a computer-animated intro movie for a video game. They all continued watching the screen and murmuring to each other until, in unison, they noticed that the craft had left the moon and was zooming towards Earth, the landmasses against the blue gradually getting larger and larger.

Soon, the Xort had entered the atmosphere and had begun to zip quickly across the planet. It settled first on Russia. The mother bear tried to scramble together a response to the UAP, but the Xort blasted the scramjets on the runway with laser shots from its automatic gun ports. Alarmed gasps and shouts rang out at the senseless destruction. The Xort was no larger than a small automobile, but it had effortlessly reduced the Russian jets to flaming, twisted rubble within seconds.

"If you care to verify our fly-by, please take a moment to confirm and then let us proceed," continued Xotro, smiling and looking impressed at Agent One's flashy demonstration.

The General Staff members immediately used their cell phones and were able to confirm the fly-by. Their phones were ringing constantly as well, as the unprovoked Russian assault had caused a sudden global stir.

"We are at DEFCON 2; the Russians think we're attacking them! Please, stop shooting their planes," asked the General a little sheepishly.

Agent One promptly returned the Xort to the outer atmosphere upon Xotro's command, pleased with his showing off the ship. The room soon quieted down and everyone was ready to listen to what the alien had to say, now that they were convinced that the craft was indeed genuine.

Xotro's job was to train the pilots. They headed to the elevator, back up to ground level, and ran into one of the RPS battery stations on the airstrip. The humans had prepared themselves as per the instructions on the information pad he'd given the Ambassador. He faced a room of grizzled, grim-faced pilots in uniform and seated solemnly at their stations, ready to learn the information necessary to operate the Remote Pilot Station.

One hundred and fifty of the nation's best Air Force pilots had been divvied out and teamed with highly-trained marksmen. As each Xort ship would need to be flown by a pilot and could support several more gunners, typically, two or more soldiers were set to work with each pilot for the training session. These men were brave and hardened soldiers, but they were still tense about the situation on their planet and felt uncomfortable at the aliens' base, not knowing if the Devil could be trusted with their well-being. They gave him a long look as he walked into the training deck with the Ambassador and General Staff.

Xotro was unaware of their doubtful stares as he addressed them. "I am Xotro. Before you are consoles for the Remote Pilot Station. We will call it RPS1.0 for short. Using the keyboard before you, enter your name, rank, and serial number so that we can track you in the system. The objects before you are bio-morph mind-way neural controllers. Very sophisticated, you know."

The troops in the room chuckled nervously but, for the most part, kept quiet and focused on their individual screens and keyboards. They were waiting for the illusion they expected to unfold, given the briefing they had received about virtually flying spaceships with their brains.

"This is not an illusion, apes. Those who ignore their training will certainly die on the battlefield. The remote neural link with the Xort is still based on the connection with your physical body, which will suffer along with the ship you control! Now, follow the instructions in the tutorial. Each of you must complete the module to move forward in your assignment. This is it for now. Type before I blast your ass!" Xotro growled.

It took two hours for all the troops present to complete their tutorials. Based on their rankings in the simulation, which monitored their reaction speed and decision-making skills, the troops were divided into twenty wings, each assigned a wing leader. The soldiers were happy to play the simulation, which hadn't been unpleasant, greatly relieving them. They were eager to continue with the training.

"Now, apes, this is the hard part. You must give yourself over to the RPS1.0 fully so that you can have complete control over your fighter craft and gun station. Each shift of your actual Xort training is a grueling twelve hours long. The Nanos will prepare you for neural connection. Ready yourselves."

At first, it was quiet. The nearly microscopic nano-bots before the men were linked like tiny ants in a chain of thin nano-tubes. They crawled all together, slithering over the uneasy pilots' bodies until little sharp cords emerged and pierced into the flesh around the soldiers' arms, ears, eyes, and mouths. The connections were over-engineered relative to the human anatomy and rendered many needless insertion points.

The men hadn't been expecting this at all and thrashed out at the sudden pain with frightened cries. The Ambassador and the other observing military officers jerked back in shock and made as if to go up and help the writhing soldiers. Xotro shook his head and held out his arm to stop them, motioning for them to watch without interference.

The air was filled with screaming. The tubes were highly invasive as they were inserted into the blood vessels and nerve bundles of the personnel connected to the handles of the RPS seats. The system would utilize the human body as an amplifier to boost the signal to the point where they could fly the Xort ships mentally.

Most organisms naturally didn't enjoy the connection process. They would instinctively jerk away during the initial stages of the bio-essence packing; the spikes in the flesh, however, ensured that the user remained thoroughly connected to the

RPS1.0
REMOTE PILOT STATION
LEVEL 2 POPULATION V1.0

RPS1.0. The screaming continued for several minutes while the RPS1.0 calibrated the bio-morph mind-way link via the nano-tube nervous system that had just been hardwired into their spines.

The room quieted down, but some of the troops were still moaning. Their fear and discomfort had diminished as the painkillers kicked in, courtesy of the feeder tubes connected through the eyes and ears. Eventually, the entire room was silent except for heavy breathing and an electronic hum.

Xotro began to recite general explanations and instructions to the pilots. "The nano-spikes meld the users' nervous systems with the controls, thereby providing a neural gateway for your brain that has been bridged to the Xorts' on-board computer to pilot the craft in real-time. I had the Xot long-range hauler, Hug, come out to a large empty space near your system's planet, Saturn, and deploy your Xorts for flight and target practice exercises. I need to prepare all of you quickly, as the Horde raiders will be coming in successive waves, and each wave will be more challenging than the last."

The troops could not believe what they were seeing, even though they were technically looking through their mind's eye. They gasped and exclaimed audibly, leaving the Ambassador and the others to wonder what they were experiencing. Space was vast and beautiful—a black velvet canvas studded with sparkling gems of many colors. Saturn's silky gas giant body loomed on the horizon, surrounded by a floating Zen garden of glittering dust and pebbles for rings. They gazed off into the distance at the twinkling stars and planets, drifting longingly towards the beautiful scenery, unaware of how to stop or move in specific directions. The pilots were ordered by Xotro to hold their position while the gunners fiddled with the interior controls using their thoughts.

The first drill maneuver Xotro wanted them to try was a type of 'Kill Box' formation, as the humans called it. It was a classic group maneuver that was effective when used wisely. A strategic mix-up of techniques would be required to deal with the ever-changing nature of the Horde. Of the assembled fighters, Xotro was the commanding voice of ten wings of fifteen fighters each. He only had these four hundred men to field and mold into an effective fighting force. With a motley group of only one-hundred-fifty crafts at his command, this was the smallest Xort fleet that Xotro had ever had to train. Minor, tight tactics would be required to make the most of this group.

Xotro ordered the first wingspread to form one side of the Kill Box. With fifteen fighters, one side of the box could be set up. Four other squads were deployed to cover the top and bottom sides, while the remaining formed horizontal flanks. The walls of the box of fighters were spaced far enough apart so that no side would accidentally crash into or shoot the other.

Xotro had Hug launch the first drone for practice. It was a simple, small spacecraft intended for target practice. He directed the drone away from the Kill Box to a distant point on their horizon. Xotro wanted the gunners to practice moving and sighting the enemy and then locking on a target. Meanwhile, another drone had already ventured into the trap.

Xotro had directed Hug to release another one near the fighters, as it provided ample opportunity for the pilots to scope out and target it. The gunners had difficulty adjusting their sights to lock in on the target. It was lost on them how to focus like one would analogously use their eyes to see something in the distance. All the pilots were in analog mode, as they were used to flying human aircraft, and they wanted to physically twist a knob or hold a stick. Their hands jerked about in the dark to no avail. It was a transition they would have to make quickly. They needed to take their flying from a physical process to a mental one.

After a few hours of practicing, several drones had been destroyed, and the gunners were beginning to lock on and hit their targets consistently. Xotro was feeling better. There were only seven hours left on the shift.

"Xotro, you have an incoming Horde wave!" reported Agent One fearfully.

"The target practice got their attention! Their original trajectory was away from your location!" interjected Agent Zero.

"Wings—alive!" barked Xotro. He focused on holding the formation and targeting the enemy vector. He hadn't intended on drawing the Horde to their practice ground, but now they had no choice but to fight.

The maneuvers he used were similar to 18th-century military formations, except rendered as three-dimensional versions of them. The wings remained stationary, and the Horde charged them. By providing the Horde with a shape to attack, the wing leader could counter their sheer numbers with strategy and misdirection. Xotro could spend all day thinking of the countless reasons why this situation sucked hardcore, but he had a battle to fight and lose and some excuses to cook up for his debriefing.

Wing after wing was destroyed in the maelstrom of metal projectiles and energy blasts. The Kill Box maneuvers were effective, but only against a small number of the overall force. Each pilot was faced with odds of more than ten to one, with very little chance of picking a target or a formation before they were beset with a massive hail of fire from every direction.

The COMMOD and Hug slunk away from the slaughter as the Horde focused in on the Kill Box by absorbing it into their 'kill ball.' Every which way the gunners looked revealed a Horde raider that was different from the last. It was as if a 360-degree net was cast over them, just from the overwhelming numbers of the Horde, swallowing them up. While the last of the battle raged on, the crew held their line, and their heroism was recognized by all the General Staff, who saw the action from monitors in the secret base. They wiped tears from their eyes as they watched the last of the battle, and the previous pilots fell.

"Cry babies," mocked Xotro about the generals, now that he was disengaged from the Xot RPS. "You shouldn't shed tears for losers. You'd be crying all solar cycle."

The Hugmoun had deployed additional gun platforms that held the remainder of the Horde patrol at bay, bringing their numbers down in groups of dozens at a time. The raiders' next meal was their motivation, however, so they persisted in their relentless charge towards Earth. The presence of the Xot crafts and gun platforms was enough to inspire a moment's hesitation but not a halt of the Horde patrol. It just led them to believe that auspicious food was awaiting them. The Horde numbers declined as the raiders blindly sought the spoils until the guns stopped, either destroyed in retaliation or eventually drained of power.

Back on Earth, inside the RPS battery stations, the floor was a terrible sight. More than four hundred men lay on the ground. The clean white linoleum was now speckled with fresh drops of crimson blood. The users had suffered massive internal hemorrhaging caused by intense bio-essence feedback upon the destruction of their neurally-linked ships, which triggered violent waves of aneurysms. The soldiers' Soul-keys were disabled because of the electrical short, so the packets containing their neural data had no home to return to, and their souls were lost to the black of space.

All of the pilots and the gunners that had been paired with them were dead. Any first aid attempted on the men was to avail. The Staff walked around the large room, dumbfounded and heavy-hearted. This exercise had turned into a slaughter.

Xotro gritted his teeth and silently hung his head in shame, but not for the reason the humans thought. This was his sixth consecutive loss to the Horde. It appeared that the enemy would have no problem picking the Earthlings' defenses apart. The proximate intergalactic transdimensional expressway would be breached next, which would give the Horde free reign to travel to other distant galaxies and spread their devastation. Xotro was on the razor's edge, and he desperately needed to plan his next move.

5

GENITALS AND GREETINGS DO NOT MIX.

The United States had fielded hundreds of its finest pilots that fateful day and the red phone was used to make the call for the rest of the world to contribute to the pilot pool. In a closed United Nations Security Council session, the operation was decided to be turned over to the Xots.

The humans had just suffered a hugely discouraging loss, and they still didn't have the means to put up a resistance against the Horde. Although some nations raised the possibility that the invading alien Horde could have been reacting defensively, they were quickly silenced. Other, more emotionally charged delegates shouted down their concerns with unquestionable footage showing that the raiders were rampaging ever closer. China and Russia agreed to send groups of their best pilots. Still, they had reservations, considering the wreckage Agent One had thoughtlessly wrought over the skies of their countries and demanded oversight as well as on-site presence at the secret base. Tensions were high as more demands were made, counter-demands were made, and accusations flew.

Trying to quell the humans' disquietude, Xotro raised his hands and proudly addressed the generals, screaming at him in a livid panic.

"This has not been a complete disaster, as your advisors claim. In this loss, there is victory, for when you grab the Rezo's nut sack, it screams!"

The metaphor was lost in the suddenly silent room.

Xotro continued his blathering monologue, relating how they would recover from the loss, ignoring the icy glares he received. The problem was beginning to become apparent to everyone present. He was becoming more and more incoherent as he ranted on, and various delegates rose from their seats angrily to stop his babbling, with clenched fists, cursing the red Devil.

Agent Zero quickly pulled Xotro aside. "Sir, please. I have a solution that will aid this planet," he whispered. He showed Xotro a large boxy device he held in his hands. He'd just pulled it out of a large duffel bag of supplies he'd brought for the big UNSC conference.

Xotro was surprised. "Why have you not zorking mentioned this earlier!?" he demanded ungratefully.

He didn't recognize the object that Agent Zero was fiddling with; it was roughly cube-shaped, black, and had reasonably minimalistic designs with a few buttons. If the Agent had some tech that could help the Earthlings' situation, he certainly had not made it clear before.

"I have not been able to get a word in edgewise. You shut me down each time I have an opportunity to speak up!" Agent Zero spat out indignantly.

Xotro turned to greet the room again after receiving an earful from Agent Zero. He had no shame and was ready to present the room with viable new options, completely disregarding his previous failed plan. He was losing faith in the humans quickly, though, as the people in the room continued to murmur about the political ramifications of this and that or lamented their tragic loss.

"It seems that my companion here is very meek and unwilling to speak up, even with the fate of the world at hand," Xotro began.

Agent Zero cast his eyes downwards as if he were still programming the device in his hands to avoid the humans' gaze. He had made many attempts to speak up before, but Xotro was a complete Torrcinian ass. Nevertheless, he would not embarrass his leader now. It would only aggravate Xotro more.

"You, Mr. President, still have a chance at glory. You could save this world. It is the second option and the last line of defense for your planet!" Xotro finished.

Agent Zero took the cue to step in. He knew that Xotro was lying through his teeth, but there was nothing to do about it but to go with the flow.

"Generals," he began, "I must begin with a brief history. My squad came to your planet over a thousand years ago to assist with advancing your technology to get your people to the point of being able to protect yourselves from the Horde raiders. We Xots have dabbled in some of your development, with positive and negative results. Mainly, human in-fighting prevented real progress until about the last hundred years. One of our Agents was slightly unbalanced, and he went rogue. We have good intelligence that says he helped spark the Inquisition, so we bear some responsibility for some of the setbacks."

"Stop apologizing to the apes, Agent Zero," grumbled Xotro in a low voice.

Undaunted, Zero continued. "I tell you all this in hopes that you will understand that the Xots have invested much time and great resources to help your people. Now is the time to defend your system against the Horde in ways..." Agent Zero trailed off in thought.

"AGENT ZERO, get to the zorking point!" barked Xotro, very impatient, as he was irritated by the boring history lesson and all of Zero's disgusting apologies. In addition, this briefing was a closed-door session, and new snacks were not allowed to be brought in until the meeting was over.

"My day job on Earth is as the elusive chief executive officer of GAMElab. I developed the Planets in Peril game, or PIP, as many call it. The game aimed to make the knowledge we needed to assimilate into your people available on a readily accessible platform. I own all of the major game controller manufacturers, and we have embedded technology in them that will transform the controller into a neural pathway that links the operator with the RPS console." Agent Zero paused just long enough for dramatic effect. "I now present to you the home defense option!"

Agent Zero placed the device he had been cradling in his arms down onto the long conference desk and also pulled several more objects out of his duffel bag. He had to brush off some cheese crumbs from the Grek platters he'd also brought in, which Xotro had long ago already devoured greedily.

The General Staff and delegates were justifiably skeptical, for before them were three different popular video game consoles and their respective controllers—not advanced-looking pieces of machinery. Incredulous murmurs came from around the room. These were playthings for children and lonely, socially inept men.

"Why, that's just an Xcube? My grandson has one of those," one of the prime ministers scoffed.

Xotro was mortified. If it hadn't been for the Grek platters that filled his stomach and the mood moderator chip in his spine, slowly losing its pacifying influence over him, he'd already have shot Agent Zero and given the briefing himself.

Agent Zero noticed his anger but didn't care and paid his leader no mind. He said what needed to be told before they were out of time.

He continued, "The home defense system was designed to be a nonintrusive planetary defense measure that could provide flexible deployment options. The defenders can fly the Xort from within their individual homes remotely via their neural connections. No time was wasted gathering at a centralized piloting station, and no military service was required. In addition, my product—the RPS2.0—can link the user and Xort in a much more efficient, faster, and less invasive manner than the outdated RPS1.0 used previously."

Xotro glowered at Agent Zero darkly at the comment as the Agent continued.

"Earth provided me with this interesting opportunity thanks to its rich variety in metals and minerals, humankind's dexterous fingers and opposable thumbs, and the recent generations' growing interest and embrace of simulation programs for entertainment. Also, you humans have the cleanest neural connection to our Xort out of any species I have ever seen, which made my modifications and development of the RPS controllers very simple."

Agent Zero's tail waggled a little in excitement as he built up to his conclusion, and everyone's eyes were focused intently on him in anticipation. "Most importantly, you already HAVE more than enough of a trained fighting force to defend Earth! You just need to draft them in the cause to battle the Horde!"

"This is taking too zorking long. The Trot's genitals are strangling me! Get to the point, now!" grumbled Xotro irritably.

Agent Zero continued in the same empathic tone about how the humans had an advantage in this new fight. The General Staff was fully briefed on the PIP guild structure and battle tactics.

"In closing, we can only field up to two hundred thousand fighter crafts, each with a crew of up to six gunners. The reserve Xorts are stored in the long-range hauler near your moon, where the Hugmoun is currently waiting after retreat from Saturn."

The generals in the room looked at each other in surprise and wondered why they hadn't gotten this information the first time.

"As there were only four of us Agents stationed on this planet, we realized early on that we couldn't influence the Earth's governments significantly enough in the time we had. With Earth's increasingly developed mechanical and engineering abilities, however, it only needs a few nudges to move its technological scale to Level Two. We introduced the PIP game to train the populace with the tactics and strategies necessary to defend their home planet. Whether it was taken as fact or fiction, the knowledge lives on in the individuals exposed to it."

Ambassador Sisko interrupted Agent Zero before he could continue the speech.

"So, are you telling me that we wasted our pilots in that disaster of a space battle, led by that rodent-eating, foul-mouthed...!? God, man! Tell me the damn options we've got here first!" screamed the Ambassador, finally losing his cool.

"Assador, Assador," cooed Xotro in his most soothing, smoothest voice.

"My name is not Assador! It's—"

"Shhh, the Xot is trying to speak," shushed Xotro.

Agent Zero said, "We simply have to flip a switch, and the remote user can enter a code to activate the nanotechnology that will be the interface. It will be the bridge between man and machine."

"How many remote locations do we have?" the President asked from across the enormous hall, using the speakerphone.

"Approximately four million disks have been sold. At least half are in the hands of skilled guilders. We have a few things to do, however, before activation. You and the other national leaders should begin by addressing the world. Call for the guilds to assemble online and prepare for battle. I will activate the satellite link that will relay the bio-signal to the Xort fighters. We must commandeer some of your spy satellites to boost the signal. I have the greatest hopes for this planet's success," added Agent Zero.

His speech had heartened the human leaders, who hurried to begin their preparations.

7

LEARN YOUR FRIENDS WEAKNESS AND SHARE IT WITH THEIR ENEMY

Once again, the planet was glued to their information cubes, hoping to glean more news regarding the space menace. All the world's governments were tight-lipped on the details. They only offered that it was a high-speed comet cloud passing through the solar system, posing no danger to Earth. This countered news reports and the raging fire on how other countries were asked to send their best pilots to the United States for top secret training.

Ambassador Sisko and Agent Zero had managed to get Xotro into the good graces of President Engressia, with both leaders being prepped by their respective advisors.

"Mr. President, you are live in less than sixty seconds," piped the press secretary.

"Xotro, I need you to be less colorful in your speech than you normally are, okay?" offered Ambassador Sisko.

"I am not quite sure what you might mean, Assy."

"Perhaps you should avoid any metaphors that might not translate well. I am confused half the time by what you say."

"Whatever you say, Joybubbles," spat Xotro flippantly.

Xotro rolled another rodent wrap and dipped it into a bowl of root beer while he stewed over his next spate of words.

Agent Zero, sensing what was about to happen, stepped between the President and his boss. The humans were disgusted by the Xot's eating habits, and Xotro was getting ready to let loose with a string of obscenities. While Xotro was chewing his food and crunching the bones of the squalling gerbil loudly,

Agent Zero directed the President to the press pulpit and offered some tips on the Planets in Peril subculture.

"It is important that you speak with the gamer guilds in mind. They've had experience since childhood, schooled in the tactics and strategies of the game that I designed—the same tactics that we need now. They have decades of experience. They are our elite forces. They are so dedicated that they have even configured display panels representing their roles in the game. Naturally, they are very familiar with their stations. Therefore, you will have a spectrum of players, ranging from complex cooperative guild players to solo players who use a rudimentary set-up."

"Guilds, yes, I get it. Nice touch with integrating military flight strategy into our youth's game culture. At least this zero generation will come to some good," grumbled the President.

"Sir, you are live," said a panicked press secretary.

President Engressia looked down, then back up, directly into the camera. It was a practiced move that began any televised speech.

"I come to you today to announce that Earth is threatened by an alien intelligence bent on conquering our lovely planet."

The President cleared his throat and shifted uncomfortably, trying not to express his disbelief in the plan. Any person familiar with subconscious body language or neuro-linguistic programming would notice his ticks and realize that he had difficulty believing in what he was about to say.

"But, not all is lost. We have a plan to face this deadly threat! We have a friend from outer space whom you have glimpsed briefly. I will introduce you to him in a moment. Please, let my words sink in. This is not a prank or a joke," he said as he paused to breathe. He hoped Agent Zero's—the intelligent alien's—plan worked.

"Our friends from the heavens have assisted humanity for a thousand years, nudging our technology, protecting us from hostile threats. We have been under their wing for a while, and it is time for us to take our rightful place in protecting our planet," the President said, continuing to delay the main point.

He was choking on what he had to say next. He kept pushing to the back of his mind that the ridiculous speech would live on as part of his legacy. It would even be in his Presidential library after this.

"I am calling for all game players, Planets in Peril, to assemble in their guild stations on the PIP servers. Earth needs your assistance," the President proclaimed as he raised his fist above his head. "Wings, alive!"

The President motioned for Xotro to come over next to him.

"This is our friend from space, the Ambassador of the citizens of the planet Xot. I present to you, Xotro."

Xotro marched over to the President, holding a rodent roll. He had put on too much weight from all his binging and was beginning to waddle a little. His red skin glared under the harsh camera lights, and his eyes squinted from the brightness as he spoke.

"Hello, people of Earth. I greet you with open arms from the Highest Xot, the Grand Emperor Xotramantus IV, who declared that his personal guard would seed the Agents of the Protocol. I am the Lead Agent of the Second Arm, and I am here to assist with the great challenge before all of us. Mmph, mmm..."

He was speaking into the camera intently, violating all vestiges of polite society by talking as he chewed. His voice was slightly muffled by the food, and he did not care about the tail stuck between his teeth nor the sickening sounds of the sad rodent squealing and the crushed bones from his noisily chewing mouth.

"Anyways, I wanted to apologize to you sensitive apes about my last message. Your government knows what I meant. Talk to them about it, okay? Stop casting me in such a negative light on your information cubes. I just want to peacefully rub love members like you do."

The Ambassador glared at Agent Zero. He was pissed; Xotro went entirely off the script rambling about love members again.

"I thought that was a misunderstanding," the Ambassador whispered tensely to Agent Zero.

"It was," Agent Zero sighed as he motioned in vain for Xotro to look at the teleprompter.

"Why do you keep bringing those revolting food platters for him?" Ambassador Sisko asked exasperatedly. "All he does all day is eat like a pig rather than focus on important matters!"

"Trust me, Ambassador. It's better this way," Agent Zero stated. "He's much easier to get along with while shoving food in his face."

The camera crew turned down the light to reduce the glare of Xotro's shiny skin. Since he no longer had to squint from the spotlights, he became quickly distracted by a Grek platter that he spotted across the room from him.

"It is important to understand, apes, that you will undergo a transformation when you meld with our technology." He said the last bit quickly, leaving out all the essential details, as his mind was preoccupied with how to get to the food.

After Xotro finished his speech, he turned to the President and nodded. The President's ashen face went unnoticed by Xotro, who was proud of this delicate mission moment. Xotro turned to the Ambassador.

"Assy, come here," Xotro called over to Sisko, motioning for him to stand with him on camera. "I want to tell you apes about my first human friend, Assador."

The Ambassador looked up at the Xot, then at the President. Engressia also looked baffled, but he quickly gestured for him to come over. This was a live telecast, and they didn't know what Xotro would do or, more importantly, what idiocies he would say, but they would play along with him. The Ambassador reluctantly walked over to join Xotro and President Engressia in front of the camera.

"Come on, Assy," crooned Xotro. "Wait! Zorking wait! Grab that Grek platter on the table first!" Xotro barked when the Ambassador had already made it halfway to the podium.

The world was watching the Devil order the American Ambassador around as if he were a waiter. A good forty-five seconds of camera time was spent telling the Ambassador how to roll a proper rodent wrap.

"Make sure there are THREE slices," Xotro suggested in a sweetly affected voice. "I just want to tell you all that it is great that you can have friends prepare food for you."

The Ambassador walked over, his fingers gingerly holding the cheese wrap with a live gerbil in it.

"Come on, Assy, you need to dip it."

The Ambassador hesitated and then quickly dipped the end of the rodent into the only bowl on the Grek platter. The Ambassador returned to Xotro, who did not stop him this time. Xotro had a broad smile on his face.

"Thanks, Assy. You're such a great friend," he said as he put his arm around the Ambassador and started taking small, careful bites of the wrap, much to the gerbil's misfortune.

Xotro was in polite company, and he wanted to make a good impression on the people watching him on the information cube. However, after the first small bite, blood and guts gushed out messily, and Xotro had to begin slurping the meaty juices up from the animal. He tried to courteously offer the Ambassador some by waving it gently in front of his face, dripping fluids and bits of cheese over his expensive suit jacket. The legs of the gerbil were still thrashing wildly.

"A little dry. Dip it a little more next time, Assador," Xotro recommended. "But thank you. Really, you're such a nice friend."

Sisko wanted to bury his flushed face in his hands in shame. The President was pretty much in the same boat.

Now that Xotro's train of thought was lost, it was timc to wrap up the speech, "So, in conclusion, I want to thank you all for listening!"

The camera director cut off the live feed, and the room let out a collective sigh.

"Xotro Sir, magnificent flipping speech, I must say!" burbled Agent One with applause.

Agent Zero was not as thrilled. Xotro was now looking at him in expectation of some form of compliment as well, but Agent Zero responded with a solemn expression.

"Sir, I think—" Agent Zero was cut off again.

"Why are you still calling me 'Sir'?" Xotro cried out suddenly, clearly irritated.

He had been hoping that this significant event in their mission would have brought the Agent to a higher level of familiarity with him. Still, Agent Zero continued to behave with a considerable lapse of protocol. By this relationship stage, the subordinate was supposed to make the Lead Agent feel essential and connected personally by graduating to a given name basis. Xotro was expecting both of his Agents to refer to him by name, but that was a practice that Agent Zero had been unwilling to follow even after all this time.

Zorks, Zero was such a Zorrcinian ass.

COWARDS LIVE LONGER THAN HEROES

Xotro grumbled loudly in the background, but luckily, his voice was muffled behind an adjoining wall. He was sequestered to a conference room next door, yelling at the television set. The information cubes were very unflattering to Xotro in the broadcast reports. It wasn't that bad of a speech, he thought. Unfortunately, his interesting usage of English, overall rudeness, and eating the gerbil live on TV only stoked the fires of heated criticism.

He couldn't believe how much of a stink the Earthlings could make over one rodent when he knew that humans killed rodents all the time as vermin and slaughtered hundreds of species of other animals regularly as food. Such hypocritical apes.

"It was just a zorking gerbil!" he shrieked at the disapproving newscasters and interviewed citizens on the television screen. He wanted to throw something at the information cube but used the remote to change the channel instead.

One channel after another had wild speculations about the President's motivation. Many people doubted whether this was a big conspiracy where the world was being duped. Many alt-news commentators put forth that this was some kind of twisted, liberal, DARPA-funded black op. They all cited Kissinger and Reagan, as the two men had made separate but equally infamous speeches about how it would take an alien invasion for the government to seize complete power under martial law.

A few news stations showed videos of Riley cultists claiming that it was the prophesied end of the world and that people ought to cleanse their souls and make peace with their doom.

For other, more rational segments of the world, the moment was surreal. The chatter was the same, regardless of the location or the speaker. Was it for real? Was it all a joke? Some even asked, "Could this be a crazy GAMElab marketing stunt?"

The gamers all sat slumped in their seats. They no longer needed their eyes to play. Each of them stared blankly into space or had their eyes closed. Most importantly, they still had the game controllers fused to their hands from the nano-bots, ensuring a solid neural connection with the Remote Pilot Station for at least the next twelve hours. Their battle had just begun.

In homes around the world, anyone who witnessed this phenomenon freaked out, thinking that their loved ones were dead or in a coma. The governments of every country were already releasing messages on their emergency broadcast stations in various languages. The announcement was repeated on news stations and on radios over and over, stating, *"This is not a joke. Your loved ones are not dead. They are in a temporary coma. They must fight the enemy in this way. They will awaken in twelve hours."*

The external visuals revealed blackness. The Xorts were somewhere dark with no stars present, so the guilders had deduced that they were waiting in a holding pen of some sort. They were right; the ships were still in Hug's belly, awaiting deployment.

"Sir, this is Agent Zero. We have a solution."

"Stop wasting my time. I know who you are. Spit the zorking answer out already, A-GENT ZE-RO," growled Xotro.

"We have approximately three thousand of the Earth's finest military pilots ready to act. Use the new recruits to take command of the Auxiliary squads under the Regulars. The pilots will learn the tactics and strategies in the field from the gamers."

"Make it happen now!" said Xotro.

"Understood, Sir. I have to take care of some other business next."

There were several other problems to solve for the RPS pilots from in-house, but Agent Zero would need a team. He knew that there was a vast pool of technophile talent to draw from, but he needed the best of the best. He had been monitoring BBS and hacker forums on the web for the past three decades. He, more than anyone else, was aware of the veterans that lurked about since the days of ARPANET. He provided the NSA Director with a short list of the needed people.

The National Security Agency Director appointed Backus to gather the new operatives. Backus, who'd been monitoring the chatter via his own modules, had picked up on the Council's activities and directly addressed them with a proposal prepared by Agent Zero. The message calling out for technical help in the fight against the Horde was enough for the various anonymous hats to show their faces. Texts were exchanged, and Backus soon arranged a pick-up for the new operatives.

The group was gathered in the conference room, which had previously been haunted by Xotro. The spectral evidence was splattered messily over the chairs and tables of the room as puddles of soda and bloody bits of tails and snouts, which the old hats tried to avoid as they sat down for briefing.

Agent Zero directed the newly assembled group. Basically, two challenges needed to be dealt with. First, there was a need to increase input/output performance by expanding the bandwidth to deploy more Xort fighter craft. Secondly, a buffer of at least fifty kryatbytes strong was needed. It was to ensure data reliability for all the pilots when passing the packet traffic. It was a fail-safe in case of a break in the link; the players' bio-essence could be stored, and the information in their Soul-keys wouldn't be corrupted. They could rescue the pilots' souls from the buffer if their Xorts were destroyed in battle. The unfortunate Air Force soldiers who had perished previously didn't havc the luxury of this buffer, so their bio-essences had been forever lost into oblivion.

Backus broke the group down very quickly. He then assigned the work piecemeal to the other hackers who were present and then to the others as soon as they arrived. They had a vital job to do and fast.

Over the communication system, Xotro and his assigned guild leader Pork butted heads. Xotro threatened to eject Pork from the battle for insubordination, and they argued until the two found a middle ground in discussing strategy. He realized, with great surprise, that Pork actually had the same ideas as he did about asymmetrical warfare. They could find common ground in military terminology because Agent Zero had infused the PIP games with Xot strategies and jargon. In short, Xotro gave Pork a free license to direct his men while he kept the second guilde leader, Lovelace on a short leash. He didn't care much for her attitude and relgated to the COMMOD.

The COMMOD received intelligence that a Horde patrol had passed Jupiter and was streaming into the vicinity of the asteroid belt. Xotro had sprinkled the belt previously with seeker mines, and the brightness of the ensuing explosions would undoubtedly draw more raiders. This would be the onset of the invasion.

Along the belt, Xotro deployed the wings. If any raiders passed the Regulars, the Auxiliaries would be ready to counter the threat. Earth needed a miracle, and they would go through many pilots if they were to win this battle.

"Explosion of mines in sector twenty-two," reported Hug to Xotro.

Xotro ordered a wall of fighters formed in Triad style with Kill Box wings. The enemy would slam into this wall of fire, the raider in front taking the heat for the raider following. If the line broke, the Auxiliaries would clean up any breach.

An estimate of the sprawling Horde size could not be made until they cleared the belt. Too many rocks would inflate the appraisal. The Mothership was nowhere to be seen yet, but it had to be close because the raiders could only venture a relatively short distance away. The raiders triggered all the mines Hug deployed while crossing the asteroid belt. While the Horde goons scrambled about, the COMMOD computer was able to calculate an estimate of what they faced.

"Approximately half a million raiders present. The ratio is nearly three-to-one."

It was fair enough odds. If the other three hundred thousand Xorts could be activated, it would be possible to even the odds completely. Either way, it was only the first wave of the Horde.

"Pork, deploy your Baiters. It's time to draw them in. Help the raiders find your lines. We are difficult to detect, thanks to our cloaking shields," directed Xotro.

"Yes, Sir!" shouted Pork.

Steve and Bill, Pork's trusted lieutenants, were already stationed directly behind one of the larger asteroids on the edge of the belt.

"Hey, *Radix Lecti*," Bill blurted to Steve.

"What, bro?"

"Look at seven o'clock. See any movement?" Bill zeroed in on an area toward the indicated movement. Through his magnification lens, he could see a myriad of raiders under the Horde banner. Aliens on rocket bikes that looked like missiles with steering wheels and combatants strapped to blasters, all holding weapons—they were everywhere.

The aliens themselves ranged in appearance from multi-limbed humanoids to other oddities; some even sported-eyed tentacles; others appeared to be cyborgs due to the mechanical limbs that were attached to a fleshy body. Occasionally, he spotted a craft that seemed to have salvaged Xort pieces welded together, usually making one of the missile-shaped bikes. The larger ships ranged in appearance as well. It was a patchwork army of vagrant races with pieces of hijacked technologies.

Bill and Steve determined that the variety of odd vehicles and weapons had once belonged to their unfortunate victims.

They were beginning to understand the nature of the Horde. They waited, silent and completely still, for some of the enemy soldiers to pass by them. Soon, enough raiders had passed, and it was time to steer the enemy towards the Kill Box.

The brothers had already planned their move and were ready to execute it. Steve moved the Xort towards the front of the pack. Bill waited for him to finish before firing into the swarm. If the raiders fell for their trick, they would head into the Kill Box.

The moment was right. The Xort moved into position. The craft had not been spotted yet. It was now merely a matter of Bill letting loose with the trigger. He used his laser cannon to shoot at several of the larger craft. Of the four shots, two hit their target, destroying the small ship and their grotesque riders. The raiders knew them, closing in with mad war cries and chants. Though the humans couldn't hear the enemy wailing, they did it for their own sake, screaming into their communicators to rile up their troops to hunt down and kill the sneaky sniper. Steve breathed deeply and held his position until the raiders were practically on top of them.

The brothers immediately punched it, and the Xort blasted off among the invaders. The chase was on, and based on sensor readings, they were being closely followed by tens of thousands of raiders. Steve continued to hightail it to the Kill Box while Bill radioed ahead. It was a matter of minutes before they closed in, and they knew that if they flew into the box to lure the raiders in with them, there was a severe chance of friendly fire taking them out as well.

"About fifty thousand raiders, based on the heat sensor readings," reported Bill to the other Tigers. "We have less than forty thousand miles to the kill line."

Steve did the only thing he could do, and he concentrated on flying forward and dodging the blaster rays that darted around the Xort. Although the cloaked Xort was hard for enemies to detect, the hot glow of the engines in swift flight provided a target for his pursuers. This was definitely different from the game.

"Steve," Bill called out anxiously, "the number is growing. Up to one hundred fifty thousand are following!"

Within moments, they'd entered the Kill Box with the raiders on their tails. The Horde of barbarians veered in all directions, shooting madly to avoid the fire, but the box formation did its job. Raider after raider fell in the Pork's unrelenting barrage. Their rocket bikes exploded with each shot, littering space with shrapnel, smoke, and limbs. It was not just the Horde that suffered casualties, however.

Pork's Xorts suffered heavy losses even though his men inflicted much damage. The rear wall of fighters took the brunt of the impact as the raiders slammed into it while tearing its desperate way out of the trap. Enzo's Regulars, along with the Auxiliaries, began destroying raiders in the frantic crossfire.

Finally, of the hundred thousand-plus swarm that had followed Steve and Bill, only ten thousand or so remained, and the Auxiliaries on the flanks tore the rest of the raiders apart. If any enemy survived, the number wasn't even worth counting. The humans had survived their first onslaught.

"Pork, report back!" buzzed a thrilled Xotro. The young man's trap had worked impeccably; on his first try, he'd organized a ragtag crew to successfully destroy a hugely outnumbering veteran enemy group. He'd found the perfect Leader to take his place in battle command.

"Pork, come in!" repeated Xotro.

No reply was received.

"Enzo, report in," barked Xotro instead, desperate to find out where Pork was.

"Presenteeeee!" giggled Enzo, still high on the thrill of the fight and the adrenaline rushing in his bloodstream. "Give it to me, Goat Boy, baby!"

Feeling thoroughly offended by the boy's nickname, Xotro wasted the next minute trying to convince him to fly into the Horde before he moved on.

"Bill and Steve!" called Xotro next.

"Present," echoed the brothers.

"I want a battlefield assessment. I have numbers here that show your wing has lost over fifteen thousand fighters. More importantly, I want you to take Pork's place."

The computer had already reported to Xotro that Pork's ship was missing in action; it couldn't be signaled at all. The battlefield assessment showed that the left flank had sustained the least damage, and Pork's group had taken the biggest hit. He was most certainly dead.

The story was not significantly different for the Iwantani guild, which had also been battered by a large part of the swarm. Hopper's Hackers held their line beside Iwantani and suffered losses just as significant. The Ruze guild had been entirely obliterated, having fought valiantly to the last craft. Over two hundred thousand raiders plowed into their Wall formation after breaching the Iwantani-Hacker line. The initials couldn't help but be overrun by the outnumbering enemies.

Still, the humans won their first battle, hands down. The apes and their progress impressed Xotro. He was almost proud of them. Despite their low technological level and never having served any real military time, they had done quite well with the Xot weaponry at their fingertips. He could see now that the Earthlings actually had a fighting chance to succeed in the war against the Horde. Xotro knew better than to be overly optimistic, though. Suddenly, Agent Zero chimed in, interrupting his thoughts.

"Sir, a second wave is approaching. It appears that the gun platforms stationed between Mars and Pluto are no longer operational. Every single one has either been destroyed or run out of power. Fourteen hours before engagement and counting."

"Give me a while, Agent; I'll get back to you," replied Xotro. He radioed into the command module, where Ada waited. "Lovelace, you're up."

"Really, Coach?" replied Lovelace sarcastically.

"I have another task that must be accomplished. The COMMOD should be ready for flight now, so get out there to support your fighters. You're the Leader of the Happer's Haklers. Show me that you can make it."

"Gee, thanks for the vote of confidence."

In an instant, the buffer space within the COMMOD increased. Redundant processes that cluttered the memory bank were eliminated, and the screen showing the battlefield, which had been fuzzy all the while, was now suddenly clear. Lights within the COMMOD brightened, machines whirred and hummed to life, and panels everywhere all turned on inside her mind's eye.

"Computer, give me a status report," ordered Lovelace.

"Two hundred thousand Xorts deployed. Fifty thousand are still operational. Eighty-five thousand under repair-bot shutdown."

The casualties were staggering. How many of her friends and coworkers had been killed here? She dreaded the answer, but she had a duty to find out. "List guilds lost," requested Lovelace next.

"The following units have suffered losses exceeding ninety percent. Guilds: Ruze, Zuse Zeus, Iwantani, Hopper's Hackers, Tigers, Torvald's Freegans, Turing Cryptobots, Well of Poes, Kilbies Killers, Noyce's Raiders, the Jack Douglas Mousers..."

Some of the names she knew well, and others were more unfamiliar; regardless, each guild name stated was a stab in the heart. The computer's list went on and on, citing great guilds from all over the world until, at last, it was finished.

Backus and his group had a clear understanding of the technical interface shortcomings between the Xot and Earth-based technologies. Their team, in addition to a network of the globe's best programmers, cryptographers, and IT professionals, pored over the vital tasks at hand. As one problem was solved, however, another one would take its place.

The biggest issue was that the bandwidth needed expanding, or the Earth would be screwed; they had to increase the RPS2.0 server's bitrate in the next several hours to get fresh Xorts deployed and pilots trained. They urgently needed more fighters out there. Otherwise, the battered guild forces would be hopelessly flooded by the new wave.

In many cases, the routing of the guild members' data was hampered by areas of low power, patchy connections, or low-speed connection. It was estimated that the average guilder experienced a latency of at least a half second—a lag significant enough to lose any edge, even in a fairly matched fight.

Though Xotro certainly wasn't one to instill the humans with any confidence in the Xots, Backus trusted Agent Zero's advice. That alien seemed to have a good head on his shoulders—the only genuinely competent one. He also felt that Agent Zero wasn't exaggerating when he'd said to the group that the Xots had been influencing human progress for over a thousand years. While working with the other programmers, he'd noticed similarities between Xot and Earth coding and algorithms.

One issue they had to deal with was the use of encrypted "Soul-keys," a two-key security feature designed to prevent wayward bio-essence packets from entering the wrong body. The bio-essence packet was encoded with one-half of the key, and the individual's DNA was the other half. Combining the two opened the switch to allow the bio-essence to return to the bio-unit. It was a complicated and delicate undertaking; if too many packets swamped the buffer and crowded the mind-way, there could be severe lags or mix-ups in the bio-essence flow. The packets had to flow uninterrupted, or else they risked becoming corrupted. Everyone on the Soul-key project shuddered at the thought of the consequences of a botched bio-essence signal flow—the pilots' souls could be lost, switched, merged, damaged, or otherwise.

LIFE IS OVER WHEN YOU DIE

Meanwhile, at the secret base outside Washington DC, there was even more tension than usual in the air. The Ambassador was engaged with Xotro.

"The President is open to all ideas," relayed Ambassador Sisko as he put out his smoldering cigarette. He'd quit smoking years ago, but now was just the time to take it up again; it might be Earth's last day, after all, not to mention everything he'd seen and been through in the past twenty-four hours.

"You have countermeasures that will only delay the inevitable. The Horde has to be stopped here. You have no choice," said Xotro, shaking his head. "However brutal the Horde may be in space, you can expect them to be a hundred times more barbarous and vicious should they manage to touch upon your planet's tender soil. You have no idea the atrocities they would commit."

"As I understand it, you say we must win in space. What countermeasures should the President at least consider if the raiders should reach Earth?" asked Sisko again.

"Well, first, widespread distribution of cyanide. Or preferably, other poisonous pills that render your body's flesh unpalatable or toxic."

The Ambassador gave Xotro a disbelieving look. "What? You're offering mass suicide as the first option?"

"Yes, otherwise, you'll just live to feed the Horde another day—brutally murdered or enslaved—most likely, not even enslaved for long. A soft, fleshy species like you Earthlings would probably be slaughtered for organ harvest or meat within the first month," said Xotro nonchalantly.

"I dare ask what the second measure would be, Lead Agent Xotro? Let me guess. Blow up the planet?" Sisko asked him sarcastically, naturally displeased with Xotro's negative spiel of fatalistic gloom and doom.

Even though Ambassador Sisko wasn't convinced, Xotro had experience with these matters. He'd seen firsthand the horrors of the Horde and what they would do to helpless victims. He sounded severe now.

"Just as drastic. I would honestly suggest you round up as many healthy children as you can for possible planetary relocation via our ships because the worst is about to come. Now, go bug your friend Agent Zero, wherever he is. I have a speech to give."

Xotro turned away from the silent Ambassador and entered the briefing room. He was still the de facto Commander despite his previous failures. The group looked to him for their next step. Agent Zero quickly pulled Xotro aside as he stepped into the room.

"Sir, the people here follow religions and philosophies to guide themselves through moral and existential crises. As they are very upset about the possible demise of their planet, it might help if you shared some inspiring words with the crew," he suggested. "Also, many generals are still unnerved by your 'glorious' horns, bright red skin, and cloven feet."

Xotro waved his hand at the Agent in dismissal. "Yes, yes, I know what I'm doing, Agent Zero. Stop worrying. You're more fretful than a mother rodent in a Grek feeding ball!"

Agent Zero stopped and let his Leader walk up to the briefing room podium, though he doubted anything Xotro had to say was very helpful. Earth was on the brink of disaster, and what its leaders and fighters needed was a good Commander to believe in and rally around during the upcoming battle. He dreaded what stupidity and obscenities might escape from Xotro's mouth this time.

"Silly younglings still holding onto your existential teddy bears," Xotro quipped into the microphone, tapping it several times.

Those present in the room stared directly at him gravely.

"Take a second to quash your fears. Give some thought to your peculiar false idols and crude deities," he declared as he bent down to roll another wrap.

The military leaders and politicians in the room had just about had enough of the harebrained fat glutton Xotro and his condescending tone. Before they could jeer him off the stand, however, Xotro continued.

"Anyways, Earthlings, I have decided to step down and relinquish the title of Commander to the human known as Ada Lovelace. She has shown the capacity to lead your planet in battle against the Horde. Listen to her as you would have listened to me, if not better."

Xotro walked away from the podium while he focused on quietly chewing on his rat wrap. He gave his cue to Lovelace via the viewing screens to the command module. They would hear what she had to say to her fighters through the briefing room's intercom.

The people in the briefing room saw through the viewing screens that the troops were splitting up and grouping as commanded. The wounded Xorts were circling the COM-MOD, protecting the Commander, and waiting for their turn for repairs. The guild wings were now spaced out again in a proper fashion.

"ALERT, ALERT, ALERT," beeped the console loudly. The sensors had detected a large swarm just beginning to pass the halfway point between Jupiter and Mars. Half the Xort ships in orbit were under queue replenishment for the deceased players, and very few of the vessels were fully repaired. There were far too many damaged crafts and not enough repair-bots to go around. She would have to order the squads out, healed as they were currently.

"Squads One to Three, move to starboard flank; remain stationary; continue repair cycle. Go!"

This command sparked a blur of activity. The queue reloaded the empty Xorts with pilots and gunners, and within minutes, the squads had moved. She planned to withdraw the remaining Xorts so that they could fully heal, and then they could be held in reserve. A smaller version of the wall was now in place between the Earth and the Moon.

"Commander Lovelace!" shouted Lt. Grace from HQ. "On the horizon, we are detecting two huge crafts. According to Agent One's analysis, one is the enemy Mothership, and the larger one in front is something else, but we have no idea what it is. The Horde is also larger than previously estimated."

"That's all we need. Continue monitoring," replied Lovelace.

"The two crafts are heading away from the COMMOD. The larger ship appears to be hauling the other and heading for Earth," Grace reported with audible tension in her voice.

On Earth, back at the office in the secret D.C. base, Lt. Grace used the Xot surveillance net to monitor the incoming Mothership. Many of the surveillance cameras that Xotro and Hug had deployed had been destroyed by Horde raiders, reducing their ability to view the enemy army. Lt. Grace angled the joystick and pressed a red button to zoom in on the large ships heading their way. She finally had a good angle from a close enough camera to get a decent look at what was coming. From within a swarming cloud of countless Horde warriors, she could catch glimpses of the large ships protected inside.

A fearful shiver ran down Agent Zero's spine when he saw what the mysterious large craft finally was. He'd been monitoring the screens as well, and he could discern enough detail now. The tugging craft was clearly a Xot long-range hauler—the Xocrowther, the Hugmoun's sibling ship. His heart sunk deep into his guts. The ill-fated Agents of the Protocol of the First Arm must have failed.

He knew those Agents from the academy. They'd spent years training together, eating cafeteria slop, and being stationed on frigid moons and uncharted planets before they had gone their separate ways as Agents into different Arms of the Protocol. This blow hit him personally. Agent Zero reported the awful finding to Xotro before his deployment in the RPS. He walked over to Xotro and solemnly pulled him aside.

"Sir," he said gravely. "We have a situation. A Xot long-range hauler was spotted in the Horde's control. It's the Xo-crowther. It is hauling the Mothership behind it. We could not pinpoint them initially because of the millions of Horde fighters surrounding them. But it is now apparent that your weapons platforms disabled the Mothership, which is why the Horde has been approaching so slowly and is forced to pull it with the hauler. Good work, Sir."

Xotro just sighed. The flattery didn't mean anything to him anymore. He looked to the ground, and he looked to the side, but he did not look at Agent Zero.

"I have to brief you on the developments of late, Agent. As you know, I am on a long string of losses, and the sighting of Xocrowther only confirms that the Protocol has failed. We have to follow the final step."

"Sir, I am staying behind," interrupted Agent Zero, standing straight and facing his boss with intent.

"Do what you will. I leave the choice to you. You do understand, however, that Agent One and I will be following Protocol if the line falls?"

"I understand the risks, Sir. But the humans have grown on me."

"I'm leaving Hug for your escape if you take it. I suggest you also prepare Hug's living quarters appropriately if you want to save a few thousand of your Level 1.9 friends," smirked Xotro darkly. "I have other priorities to consider now, and these apes are low on the list. Agent One will accompany me as my Scapagot to shave my heels and trim the hairs on my legs and nether region."

"Good journeys, Xotro," bade Agent Zero as he turned back to busy himself with the flashing consoles beside him. This would be the last time they saw each other. He was glad to be rid of that asshole.

Xotro noticed Agent Zero had used his real name for the first time in his farewell. He was momentarily stunned and speechless, moved by the gesture. Finally, when the moment passed, as all moments do, he turned and motioned for Agent One to follow him.

His exit needed to be swift and quiet, even if the humans were currently listening to Lovelace and Agent Zero. He didn't want to panic the humans. He had a new mission to complete, and the apes were still under the impression that they really had a chance. Xotro had Agent One load their provisions onto their light cruiser. There was no time to check the manifest. It was less than three scant hours before the Horde was expected to reach the last of Earth's defences.

"No freeze-dried rodents for this trip, Agent One," stated Xotro, entering the spaceship.

Agent One was at the controls, awaiting his order to depart. He smoothly guided the scout ship out of the underground bay just as the doors closed with a "whump" below them. Xotro was greeted by Hug as soon as they had docked their cruiser on the outdoor landing strip.

"Good day, Xotro. Glad to have you back," politely intoned the automated vehicle.

"Shove it, Hug. Agent One and I are leaving this hell-hole in the light cruiser. Just remember to fuel the ship and perform preventive maintenance. Have its departure ready within two hours."

"Right away, Xotro, but we are in the middle of planning for the upcoming battle. I really should focus on deploying Xorts to the field as soon as orders come in from Commander Lovelace," the Hugmoun replied meekly.

"No one told you to stop deploying. You just have a higher priority to take care of right now. Put the Xorts in the field when you can afterward. I have other matters to take care of. Get out of my business," growled Xotro irritably to the sensitive ship.

"What shall I do without you?" asked Hug.

"Agent Zero is your new codependent. Glom on to him instead."

"Yes, Xotro. Nice serving with you, Sir. Your ship will be ready in less than two units." Despite being an artificial intelligence, even Hug was, in his own way, glad to be rid of Xotro.

Xotro had begun to ignore Hug again. He focused on shouting at Agent One, "Why have you not loaded those damn crates yet?"

Agent One started to regret his decision to come along, but he didn't really have much choice in the matter. Xotro stormed off to some other part of the ship, and Agent One paused to reflect on everything that had happened in the past two days. He gazed out of the port hole silently, watching the bustle of activity outside. People hurried back and forth; military trucks carried soldiers and supplies to and fro. The humans were scared, scrambling, trying their hardest to protect their home.

Judging from the screens in the cockpit of the cruiser, which were playing live feed from the surveillance cameras that Xotro had deployed, the humans had been doing a decent job holding the Horde off in the rocky asteroid belt between Jupiter and Mars—the vast divide between the outer and inner planets. If the raiders managed to fight through the ninety million-mile belt, Earth would be a mere hop, skip, and jump away. With the incredible size of the approaching raider army and their bringing the stolen Xot long-range hauler and Mothership, he knew that the Horde was sending everything they had against the humans' defenses. They were traveling on a one-way ticket; it was Earth or Bust.

Back at the forefront of the battle, Bill and Steve suggested to Commander Lovelace to execute a reverse Trail maneuver. They badly needed more Xort repairs and needed to buy time. Echoes of Pork's tactics panged against Ada's mind as they made the suggestion. Naturally, they would suggest his sorts of tricks, as they were members of Pork's guild. Though not a Tiger herself, she was familiar enough with Pork's strategies that she knew that when they said "reverse Trail," the plan was for the Horde to be distracted by the COMMOD. Forty percent of their force was still in need of repair, and she would give the Horde an irresistible and easy Trail to follow.

Steve and Bill deployed the Bait. They'd directed the rest of the Tiger guild to various roles behind the line. The squad that served as the Bait for the Trail was now spread far enough apart to create the illusion of a path of 'bread crumbs' for the raiders to home in on and follow.

"Lovelace, the line is up," reported Bill. He and Steve were prepared to respond to any threat with their wing, which was fifty thousand strong.

The wounded Xorts moved along with the COMMOD behind the dark side of Mars, the last planet before Earth. She maintained her stand before the barren red world, teeth clenched and white-knuckled.

Mars was named after the god of war—a poignant thought to her. She hoped it wouldn't be a bad omen. She braced herself. The stretch of the Trail ended at her position, leading the raiders to the COMMOD. She was alone at the end of the line. Undefended.

The Horde had dispatched a wing twenty-five thousand strong, aiming to crush the COMMOD. Lovelace staggered as the ship rocked violently and lights flickered. She was shocked

at how quickly they had gotten to her. She attempted some evasive maneuvers, but a wing had been clipped by raider rail guns. They filled space with the hot lead, ripping through any ship in its path. It was almost impossible to dodge all of the streams of bullets. It was a matter of luck whether anyone could avoid the fire. She responded by hitting the thrusters and firing back madly, killing some of the pursuing raiders but not nearly enough of them. The COMMOD's round banks were soon emptied of their ammunition, leaving her station completely defenseless.

The diversionary game had taken a turn for the worse as she became swarmed with enemies, whooping and taking potshots at her ship. Nearby Xorts tried to help alleviate the situation by strafing the enemy mass in fly-by, but their efforts were too feeble. A few Horde members would break off to shoot them down or otherwise chase them off but then go right back for Lovelace's throat. They were focused and out for her blood.

"Help!" cried Commander Lovelace desperately.

She was unable to rotate out, and no one could queue in. The hackers at home had stabilized her connection to the remote system while the government had directed medical help to her location to try to keep her alive.

The battle damage was taking its toll. Her body, still sitting on the sofa in her living room, jerked a little; her nerves were firing, and her muscles twitched. She was suffering nosebleeds and twinges of pain in her head that she thought might be tiny aneurysms. Paramedics hurriedly placed an oxygen mask over her nose and mouth. Even though her heart was beating rapidly, her blood pressure was dangerously low, and her tissues weren't getting enough oxygen. Her mind is far away in the heat of space conflict. She didn't even feel it when the paramedics slid an intravenous needle of saline and packed red blood cells into the crook of her arm. A thin trickle of blood oozed down her face and dripped off her chin, staining her flower-print couch.

Back in space, the ship jolted again. Lovelace tried to get the ship moving to buy herself and her troops more time, but everything was getting dark and spinning. She was going to die. Just as her vision began to fail and she thought it was over, the swarm began to act erratically around the COMMOD.

A lone Xort fighter had burst into the Horde cloud, causing major havoc. Its gun ports fired from all cylinders—one true shot after another. The craft could only be detected by its laser's burning glow before it blew up a target. The reckless Xort fighter cleared a direct path through the swarm's center like a hot knife slicing through butter.

The ship's operator understood the perfect balance of shields, stealth, and weapons. Targets were dead as soon as they were sighted. The undisciplined groups of raiders panicked as they began shooting at each other, snarling angrily and trying to hit the marksman ghost. Soon, the entire swarm was ignoring the COMMOD.

With a little bit of help from a few flankers, the swarm patrol was eventually reduced from their original twenty-five thousand strong to nothing more than sizzling space rubble.

The bold Xort darted in front of the COMMOD, and an obnoxious voice that wasn't hard to recognize rang out, "Ha! I'm back."

"What," choked out Lovelace, puzzled. "I thought you were dead?"

"Well... Let's just say the geeks on the ground did the trick. My bio-essence is temporarily residing in this Xort ship. This is my soul's new home until they can transfer me back out," Pork explained.

"But, I know you're dead," Lovelace unquestionably replied. "I got a report earlier saying that you had a massive heart attack when your original Xort was destroyed. Your body's gone... Basically, you *are* home now."

Pork took an instant to think before he replied. "Whatever… Ghost in the machine, maybe? Wu Pang rises from the dead?" he joked offhandedly.

"Do you know Asian anecdotes for every situation?" Lovelace retorted, her spirits lifting. It was as if Pork's soul had returned from the dead. She wondered how many people the tech crew at home had been able to save in this way. Maybe everyone's bio-essences had been salvaged.

"As to strategy, yes. Look at it as Musashi against the many. Always outnumbered and outmanned. Yet, he always chose the right target at the right time with the right move; it was brilliant. The five steps to victory. You couldn't find an old-fashioned western that could provide such an inventive stratagem."

"I guess it does speak to the few against the many. I can offer The Magnificent Seven one of these days," proposed Lovelace.

"More like the Seven Samurai," replied Pork. "I'll friend you, and we can discuss this more over some late-night IMs... I could teach you a few things," gloated Pork. If the Xort he was residing in could wink, it would have.

"Enough with the chatter; you must get COMMOD back to Earth! The rest of the swarm is headed there! We must take out the long-range hauler and the Mothership!" bellowed Agent Zero.

"Roger, Roger," replied Pork. "I'm going to head back to Earth and do as much damage as possible!"

Pork's ship burst away and straight into battle. After all, he was already dead anyway. He hungrily sought out the Mothership, which was in range. He could be heard over the com by everyone, laughing like a madman, zipping about the battle, popping heads, nailing raider after raider. His weapons array had enough charge to do quite some damage to their Mothership, he imagined. His craft bounced about, mimicking Enzo's quirky squirreling habit. Despite the raiders' defensive barrage of fire, his Xort remained on target—aiming directly for the Mothership's bridge.

The tip of Pork's Xort pierced the Mothership's energy shield.

"Long live the Pork! Aaahhhh—" And there was no more.

Pork had fired his entire bank of weapons into the ship's bridge a split second before his craft crumpled and smashed through the plated windows of the bridge. The explosion ripped through the passage, spreading shrapnel and fire to all decks of the Mothership. Flames spread through every nook and cranny and quickly licked into the generator room. Few raiders could escape the smoldering cauldron as the generator exploded and the internal pressures blew the rest of the Mothership to smithereens.

Meanwhile, at the secret base outside Washington DC, Agent Zero estimated that based on the density of the mass, the Horde army had been reduced to less than half of its original size and located halfway between Mars and the Earth. This was evidenced by the brief two-second light show of the last of Hug's mines detonating the fuel-laden rocket bikes of several unlucky raiders. The fireworks served as a grim welcome banner, announcing their arrival in the area.

Agent Zero could hear Backus on the communications in the background, excitedly summarizing their progress to Lt. Grace and the others.

"So, the solution occurs in two steps: a bio-essence safety buffer auto-activates when a Xort fighter is mortally damaged, and then the bio-essence resides within the memory banks of an unoccupied Xort fighter upon the original Xort's destruction. Their Soul-keys would be uncompromised and intact."

The Xot Agent was impressed with the humans. In the short time they had, they had used their ingenuity to cleverly work out a method to keep their pilots from losing their lives in the RPS. Necessity, with a healthy dose of sweaty-palmed desperation, was undoubtedly the mother of invention.

With the main task of finding a way to save the fighters' souls successfully dealt with, Lt. Grace and Backus stood on

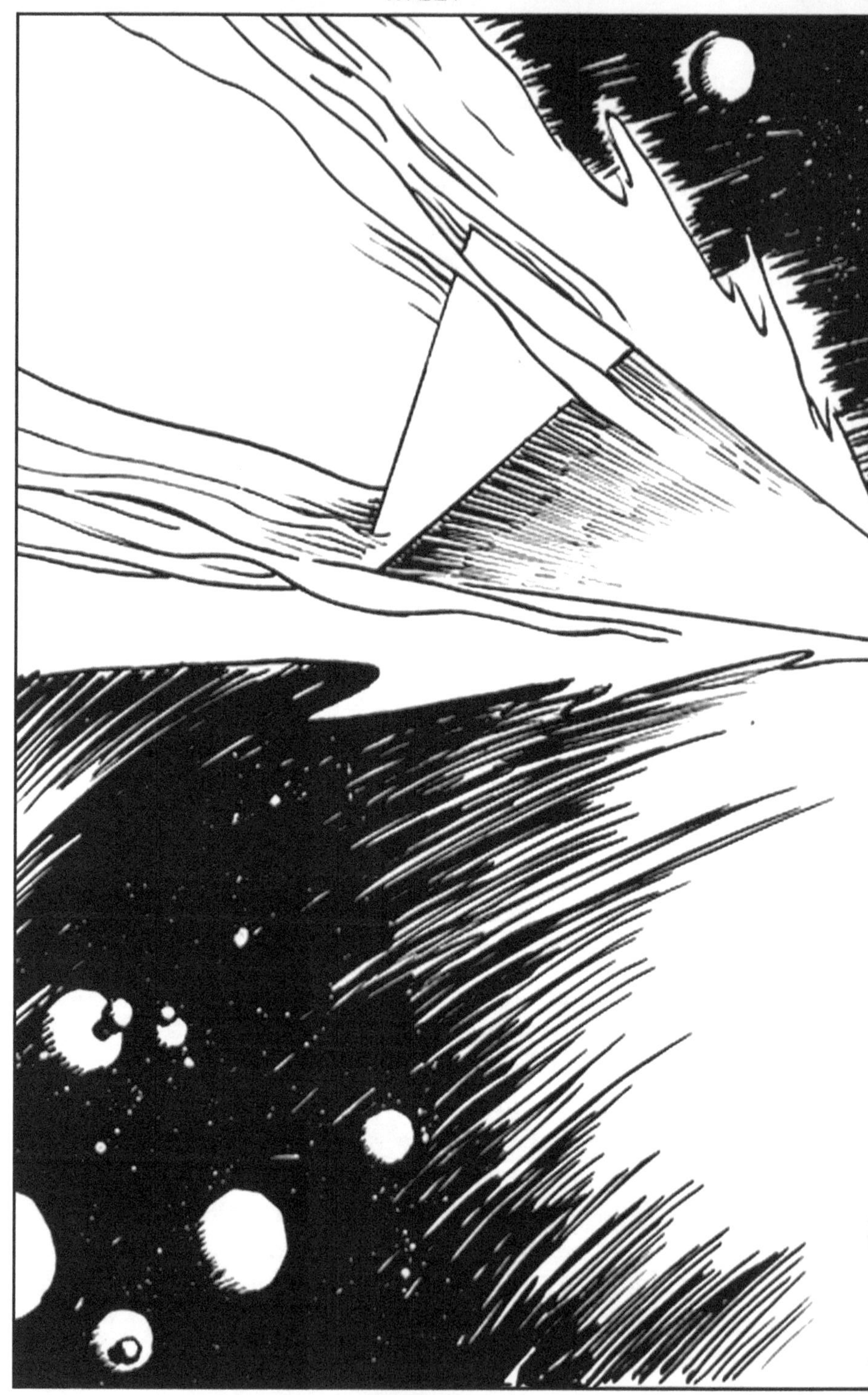

the steps outside of the office, watching the fireworks in the night sky as they held hands. The fight had come to Earth's front door. Everything was now up to the guilders.

The flashes of light in the heavens above them gradually grew brighter, and the reverberations of exploding ships grew louder as the frenzied fight drew closer to Earth. Not knowing whether they would live or die, the two were going to spend what could be their last few minutes enjoying each other's company. Backus was secretly hoping to have sex but kept the thought to himself. Similarly, Lt. Grace hoped that some sparks would fly, but she wasn't too keen on the idea of losing her virginity—already five times removed—with someone she didn't know all that well yet.

Since the two had begun hanging out together in the compound, they'd grown closer, and they both knew that it was an excellent time to act on their instincts. Something in the tender moment made Lt. Grace want to know his last name. She opened her mouth to ask, but just then, Agent Zero called them to urgently return inside the building.

"After you saved Pork, he returned to battle and smashed his Xort into the Mothership. It blew up."

"So, that's what the explosion was," commented Lt. Grace, remembering the distant sound.

"Yes, we believed he was truly dead this time, but he resides in the COMMOD. Lovelace sacrificed herself by pulling him out of the Xort and rotating with him at the last second. She made the Commander's choice. We are pretty sure she died when Pork's Xort hit the bridge of the Mothership."

Backus and Lt. Grace looked appalled as Agent Zero explained the situation to them.

"We don't know if the new buffer sucked her bio-essence packet out in time. She is lost in the buffer. Go and find her. We don't have much time.

Despite his heroic actions, which Pork had thought would have been his last, he was back in the battle. However, he was now in the COMMOD rather than in a Xort. Obviously, Lovelace had done something—hopefully not something stupid. He was stunned but shook it off and focused on the fight before him. The long-range hauler was still heading for Earth, cram-packed with angry, homeless raiders onboard. He was now Commander, in charge of the COMMOD, as he had always wanted. It didn't come with the glory, cheers, and fanfare he had always imagined, but that didn't matter anymore. He was ready to kick some alien butt.

"Agent Zero! One medium-sized incoming object coming in fast, and it's unidentified," reported Pork.

"Feed me information as you receive it. We need to find out if this is friend or foe," responded Agent Zero. In a second, he smiled when he realized what it was.

Xotro had returned.

"Everyone, back away from the hauler as fast as you can!" the Lead Agent shouted to the troops as he tore by.

He was focused on the stolen long-range hauler. It had been pulling the enemy Mothership when Pork crashed into it and had been severely damaged from the ship's explosion, so now was the perfect time to attack. The impaired Xocrowther crawled along slowly; it was scorched and dented, and smoke plumed out all along its battered surfaces. He had a plan and decided he would buzz Agent Zero later and apprise him of the situation after he had dealt with it.

Xotro left the shields of his cruiser turned off to go in complete stealth mode as he jetted into the thick of the swarm. The Horde parade was just passing the Moon when Xotro triggered a modified bomb targeting the vicinity near the long hauler.

The bomb exploded, and, as he expected, the Xocrowther slammed lengthwise into the rocky satellite. His plan to use the concussive force of the bomb to crash the compromised long-range hauler into the dusty grey Moon had worked. It was pure luck that the Horde happened to cross nearby enough that Xotro had been able to use the Earth's Moon in his improvised plan. He urgently wanted to get his hands on the stolen Xot ship to learn what had happened to his comrades in the First Arm and how they could have been taken by such a lowly adversary.

An added bonus to his guile was the enormous rumbling blast that took out many raider rocket bikes and their hijacked patchwork crafts with its wake. It was easy to see that the vast majority of the remaining segments of the Horde army had been destroyed. A pathetic medley of stragglers managed to survive and relentlessly continued towards Earth. It was still do or die for the last handful of raiders.

The humans and Xots would make sure that it was the former.

Bill and Steve led the balance of the troops at the wall. The exhausted and demoralized raiders were dispatched quickly with great cheering from all.

On Earth, all the hats and generals and Presidents, as well as the rest of the whole world, celebrated. Prime ministers wiped tears from their eyes; journalists prepared their following joyful articles; engineers at NASA threw up their papers like confetti; bubbling champagne bottles were popped open; even the techs at the server farms cried and hugged despite their smelly sweatiness and scanty clothing.

While listening to the happy noise in the background from his headset, Xotro parked the cruiser by the beached hauler and did a quick survey of the sad, smoking Xocrowther. He was not ready to make merry quite yet.

Inside the captain's deck, by the freshly dead and mangled bodies of some Horde barbarians, he found the body of a poor fellow Xot with crude stitches on his head from a vulgar and unwilling surgery. His brain had been replaced by a slave core after they'd sucked his knowledge out.

Hug confirmed that the ill-fated Xot captain, in his last act, had put the Xocrowther's AI into hibernation once the raiders had taken the vessel hostage, which was good because Xotro could now review the deceased Lead Agent's log. It appeared that the Horde had, therefore, been unable to use the Xorts in the hauler, as the bay was still full. It was stocked with Xort craft and battle bots in various states of mostly great disrepair. After assessing the logged information from the hauler, he had an announcement to make to everyone on Earth.

Xotro appeared on the massive monitor back at the base.

"You're back, Xotro!" said Agent Zero, smiling broadly.

"Yes, well, I knew you would need my help. Plus, Agent One is driving me crazy. Prepare some Grek platters for my return, Agent Zero. Also—" The signal was fuzzy and breaking up. "-it ....a .... s.... party."

"Did you hear that, people!?" shouted Backus. "The man said, 'Let's party!'"

The planet was one huge celebration. Everyone was extremely excited about the outcome of the battle. Even the tearful friends and families of the gamers who had died in the fight understood that their loved ones had fought heroically in an incredible intergalactic war to save the lives of everyone and everything they knew.

It also helped that said friends and families felt considerable comfort in the fact that the pilots weren't genuinely dead and their souls lived on in the Xort ships. In addition, it was soon announced that it would be easy for the Xots to eventually engineer robotic bodies to put the gamers' soul packets into so they could live at home with their families again.

In the end, despite the odds, the humans and the Xots had teamed up successfully to beat the Horde. No Level Two planet had ever accomplished this before. Even by Xot standards, this victory was a big deal.

Agent One docked the star cruiser in the bay of the secret base. The door closed above them as he and Lead Agent Xotro exited the spacecraft. The entire command center was rejoiced. The roar of cheers filled the room and only became louder when the two Xots walked by. Some people even began chanting Xotro's name enthusiastically, all past faults forgotten.

Agent Zero walked over to Agent One while Xotro headed to the generals milling about the central panel. Xotro faced them, and before he began his announcement, he swirled a hard object around his mouth and spit out a large rodent skull.

"Gentlemen and ladies, be proud. The cuisine of this planet is outstanding, and your fighters are quite the standard." He shifted his position to view the giant screen behind him.

"Before entering your system, I had laid down surveillance nets throughout your star system periodically." He continued to shift and toggle a joystick on the console.

Pointing at the screen, he continued, "But it was the First Arm's Xocrowther that had laid down the cameras capturing the footage here. What we have on the screen is the main Horde party ten times the size of the group you just faced. I didn't say, 'Let's party.' I said, 'It was only a scouting party.'"

The generals were dumbfounded. The lousy news somewhat dampened the spirits of the people present, but the cheerful mood was still intense. It had been an extremely long forty-eight hours. The Earthlings had beaten the Horde today, and they would be prepared to beat the space barbarians back again another day. For now, they would seize the moment and enjoy the sweetness of their victory.

Agent Zero and Agent One continued their conversation to one side of the room.

"So, why did Xotro really return?" asked Agent Zero.

Agent One shrugged and replied with a sheepish smile, "We forgot the crates of rodents."

CREATORS

ODDNESS

This reclusive person (author, publisher, producer, editor) specializes in crafting captivating short story collections, novellas, and comics that transport readers to extraordinary realms is also the driving force behind Forbidden Futures magazine, where the fantastic and the unbelievable come to life.

Originating from unknown lands, ODDNESS dabbles in composing electronic music and playing video games.

MIKE DUBISCH

This graphic novelist and illustrator has been creating and publishing comics and art since the 1980s. He has carved out a unique place creating horror, science-fiction, surrealism, and YA adventure works using all but lost traditional techniques. Born in California, USA, the artist has traveled and lived in five countries. He has been an instructor at the Academy Of Art University since 2012 and is married to children's book illustrator and sculptor Carolyn Watson Dubisch, with whom he has three daughters.

FUTURES

www.ingramcontent.com/pod-product-compliance
Lightning Source LLC
Chambersburg PA
CBHW030337310726
48979CB00001B/64
* 9 7 8 1 9 6 0 2 1 3 2 6 6 *